To: Georgia

Best wishes

Virginia Saalman

Frog Poop

and other stories

Virginia Saalman

ECITY•PUBLISHING

Everglades City, Florida

Dedicated to my husband, our children, and our grandchildren.

Frog Poop and other stories

illustrations by Erica Dykes

set in Goudy Old Style, 12/16
printed and bound in the USA
First Edition, Second Printing, March 2008

ECITY•PUBLISHING

P O Box 5033
Everglades City, FL, 34139

email: frogpoopbooks@yahoo.com

ISBN 978-0-9716006-4-5

CONTENTS

THANKS

I'm grateful to my family and the many good friends who have read, re-read, and re-read again the stories in *Frog Poop*, searching for the elusive typo or grammatical mistake.

A special thanks to those members of my family, who, as youngsters, at one time or another over the last fifty years, listened attentively to my stories of the "Kroopenpopper" Family. At long last, a Kroopenpopper saga finds its way into print as *Jack Be Nimble, Jack Be Dead* in this collection. Thanks "De" for never giving up on me or the "K" family.

Sincere thanks to my friend of many years, USDA's own Ron Hall, for reading my drafts, occasionally publishing my articles, his continued encouragement for *Leslie*, my unpublished love story, and for his wonderful response to this collection of short stories.

A special thanks to my publisher, Marya Repko, ECity Publishing, for her friendship, patience, and her amazing technical and computer expertise.

INTRODUCTION

The short story is distinctly American and has been a favorite literary form for authors and readers alike for over a century. Long before that, people told short stories as tales and fables. The definition of "short" as it relates to a story is illusive, often being described as that which can be read in one sitting. However, because people read at different speeds and a "sitting" may mean something entirely different to the retired reader than the busy executive, that definition seems inadequate. What matters most is that, in the telling, a measure of enjoyment is passed from writer to reader.

The eight stories in *Frog Poop* are of various lengths: the first four take place in the Florida Everglades; the next two are mysteries, and the last two touch upon family dynamics and emotions. The Florida Everglades are like no other place on the planet and I have tried to incorporate some of the rich flavor and history of the area in the tales that take place there.

I hope you enjoy all of the stories and perhaps will want to read some of them more than once.

Virginia Saalman
Naples, Florida
August 2006

FROG POOP

Frog: Any of numerous tail-less, chiefly aquatic, amphibians of the order Salientia, and esp. of the family Ranidae, having a smooth, moist skin, webbed feet, and long hind legs adapted for jumping.

My name is Maggie Sullivan and if my mother had told me I'd end up in the swamp helping my uncle run his small medical clinic at the end of nowhere, I'd have said she was as loony as their sister, my Aunt Nellie, who passed on years ago after spending ten years in St Elizabeth's over in Southeast Washington, not far from where I lived my life from age four to middle seventh grade.

You see, I'm a city girl, born and bred, and the closest I've been to the country or to a swamp was the year dad borrowed on the insurance policies and we all piled in the car — a Ford station wagon that had a propensity to stall in heavy traffic — and drove straight through to Disney where I rode on some contraption contrived by a maniac who thought snakes falling out of trees and scaring the beejesus out of city folks would be a hot ticket item. He got that right.

Then there was the time our fifth grade class took a field trip to southern Maryland so we could see for ourselves that chickens began with feathers and legs — not drumsticks — and not in cellophane bags at Giant or Safeway. That trip, all good educational intentions aside, also ended prematurely when Joey, the dirtiest-minded kid in our class, yelled for everyone to come and see how the donkey's "dick" almost drags the ground.

Those two life-altering events were all the "country" I needed, at least until I found myself in the offices of Dr. Goren, my newly-discovered shrink and husband of Nina, the receptionist in the hospital where I worked.

"He won't charge you much," Nina had said, "because he doesn't have many clients, you're my friend and I told him you are poor as a church mouse and about ready to go off the deep end and either kill yourself or Mark." Nina didn't miss much, especially the part about killing Mark. Oh great, so now I was going to pay half a month's salary to spill my guts to a shrink who didn't have many clients.

It only took one visit and, boy, did I ever spill my guts.

"See," I said, "I thought Mark and I were drop-dead, don't-ever-leave-me, I-can't-live-without-you happy until that evening." The drop-dead part was the only part that I had right. It was as if he were the only one affected by the loss of a baby we had tried for years to have. When I finally discovered I was pregnant, both of us were overwhelmed with joy. I guess his way of handling his grief was to withdraw from the relationship, eventually finding someone else to console him.

It was our fifth wedding anniversary; I'd picked up *Lo Mien* — our favorite — and stopped off to buy an aroma therapy candle and a CD by *his* favorite quartet. I walked into our apartment to find a note on the kitchen counter, "Sorry Maggie, I've got to go away for awhile." Awhile turned out to be forever and I didn't see him again until we appeared, with our respective lawyers, in a swank suite

— his lawyer's office, not mine — on New York Avenue. With Nina for a friend, I figured I didn't need enemies, for between the cheap shrink and the expensive lawyer, I was now totally broke and so I figured as long as I was paying for time with "dumb nuts" (that's the name I gave Dr. Goren after 15 minutes on his couch), I'd consider taking his advice which pretty much boiled down to about six words: "Get out of town, as far away as you can, for as long as you can and get past this." Well, maybe that's more than six words, but just the same, the *get-out-of-town* part played over and over again in my brain. Where would I go? Who would want to be around a pathetic, sniffling, feel-sorry-for-herself jerk?

That night I called Uncle George, my mother's favorite brother, and the person to whom I'd gone for advice after my own father had died years before. I sobbed and he listened, which was the typical way our conversations went, especially during my high school years, when he knew that advice wasn't necessary, even when early in my freshman year, I called to tell him I was madly in love with a senior, Bobby Jones, whose life ambition, after graduation, was to work in a gas station. To young teenage girls, it didn't really matter what a guy's future occupation might be; a senior with a red convertible — even missing a right front fender — trumped all else. Of course, it didn't hurt if he looked like a cross between Elvis and the man on the latest issue of Surfer's World.

Somehow, Uncle George trusted that I would get over Jones. He was wise enough not to tell me that. Just like all the other traumatic teenage episodes I encountered, I just had to cry and he just had to listen. Later, in college, I still called to cry on his shoulder but I like to think I had matured enough to actually ask for his advice, which if I had to guess, I probably followed a good three quarters of the time. The other quarter is another story and best left forgotten.

After Mark and I were married, I never again called Uncle George for advice. We did call each other on birthdays or to occasionally arrange a lunch. That all changed when I lost the baby and Mark took a powder. There I was again — the child — spilling my guts to the one person who had always been there for me. I guess even the saintliest of uncles has a limit because after about two hours he said, "Doctor Goren may not be the highest priced shrink in town but I agree with him. You need to get away and the sooner the better." That wasn't what I had expected and certainly wasn't what I wanted to hear — that I should pack up and leave.

"Where would I go?" I asked. "What would I do?"

He paused a long time before he answered. "Why not go down and help Doc? Spend some time on the water, soak up some sun — forget."

Doc was George's brother — my Uncle Edward whom I didn't know very well. For some reason, unknown to most of the family he had ditched the world of the big city a number of years before and opened a clinic in the most remote part of Florida — the Everglades. I remember that some in the family, my mother included, thought he had lost it, thought that he had inherited the same "loony" gene as his sister, Aunt Nellie.

"Forget! How in the hell can I forget," I said. "How can I forget this whole damn year?"

A box of tissues later, I said "And besides, isn't the place where Doc lives the last place on earth most civilized people want to go?"

"You underestimate the Everglades, my dear," he said. "Some people call it paradise — my brother does and also calls it his home — forever.

"Yes," I answered argumentatively, "But there are also some who call it 'hell'. I think your brother was nuts to leave a successful practice here and go to a place where smugglers and crooks hide out — not to mention a town that almost got wiped out three years ago by a monster hurricane."

"All that may be true," he said, talking to me softly as if I were still a child. "But it might be just what you need. Get away from the city, get back into nursing. Besides, Doc's shorthanded and right now he could use some help."

And so it was five days later that I, Maggie Sullivan, nurse from New York City, grieving the loss of both my husband and baby, found myself at the Ft. Myers airport waiting for a ride that would take me deep into the Everglades. I wondered what in the world had possessed me to make such a decision.

● ● ●

The Everglades. It doesn't much matter what his name was. Most folks remembered him as the hermit who lived on Hog Plum Key and by the manner in which he carried himself when he came into town to stock up on groceries, toiletries and bullets and by the unanswered questions about where he got his money, how he spent his time and where he went when he left his island late at night. Back then, most kept their curiosities to themselves. Better to let the gossipers believe what they wanted rather than ask a man direct questions about his personal life. It didn't take too many years for the line between fact and myth to become as blurred as an early morning fog over the Glades.

Unless provoked, in which case some believed he could strike fear into a six-foot rattler, he was a mild man who never caused anyone much trouble. Some thought he might be just like a lot of other men who came to the area escaping the law up North.

He had long before developed a raging fungus on his feet from being in water much of the time and, except for the years he went off to school in New York, he could often be seen outside his small house on Hog Plum Key, where he was born and raised, with both feet soaking in a bucket of bleach.

His new perfect, straight, white teeth were a huge improvement, replacing his own that had become jagged and were the color of cider from one-too-many encounters with overhanging limbs and the chaw of tobacco that rested squirrel-like in his right cheek until Doc told him he'd hate to have to operate on him for mouth cancer.

It was said that his deep blue eyes could soften and reduce a woman to sighs or they could turn the color of steel and reduce a man to quivering when a neighbor or the land had been wronged.

He had a quiet manner about him except when someone riled him, like the time when the Swift boys snuck over on their skiff to his island and tried to steal one of his pigs. No one knows exactly what kind of a licking he gave those two but, from then on, both of them brought home good grades from school and never again ran afoul of the law. In fact, it was a surprise to everyone, except perhaps to him, when those boys left the area to go off to college.

One especially cold winter night, under cover of darkness, with one bloody arm hanging limp and a deep gash running from his right brow across the bridge of his nose and down almost to his left ear, he silently guided his skiff up the river to the city dock. Weak from exhaustion, hunger and loss of blood, he managed to half walk, half crawl to Doc's house down on Main Street which served as the town's small clinic. Just before sunrise, four hours and some ninety stitches later, Doc helped him back to his boat. When he didn't appear in town for the next couple of weeks, there was speculation that he had finally been killed by "Big John", the name locals had given to the fifteen-foot gator that for years had been blamed for eating Buford Herrill's goats. If that old gator hadn't gotten him, some passed it around as gospel that he had died at the hands of fellow rifle-toting poachers undoubtedly in an argument over territory. Since some were convinced that he was a poacher himself, that explanation seemed plausible enough.

Some even speculated that he wasn't a poacher at all, but instead was the mysterious agent who was gaining a reputation for surprising and disrupting poaching operations in the islands. And when he did show in town, with the still raw red scar stretched diagonally across his face like some monster in a horror film, rumors and tall tales flew through the town like a swarm of hornets. However, none queried him and, in fact, all avoided him as if he had contracted tuberculosis.

Only Doc Johnson and old Sheriff Billingsly knew the truth. Only those two knew that after his father was killed by poachers, he took a vow that he, like his father, who unfortunately didn't live long enough to name his attackers, would defend the territory against illegal hunting of native species and had committed his life to protecting their survival.

Hunting poachers down came easy to him, unlike some of the lawmen imported from areas outside the Glades who were at the mercy of the outlaws who had also cut their teeth guiding boats through the maze of the Ten Thousand Islands. He could run across the waters at night just as fast as anyone and he knew the tides and the oyster bars by heart. He could recognize the sound of any kind of motor that approached and most often he knew who was operating it. He felt the playing field was even.

The only difference between him and them was that he had chosen one code and they had chosen another. But now, he must be more careful; his true mission was at risk.

The outlaws that he tangled with were a mix of tough urban punks and country rednecks, some of whom were ex-cons, thieves or worse. More than a few were violent, dangerous men. Disputes were not pretty.

Folks knew he had been married twice and rumor had it that both wives had left declaring that living in the interminable heat, fighting the hellacious hordes of mosquitoes and riding out hurricanes in boats on the lee side of his island were more than they had bargained for, no matter how much in love they might have been. To make matters worse, neither had known what their husband did at night when he disappeared for hours, often returning just before sunrise with no real explanation of where he had been or what he had been doing — just that he had necessary work to do and if they knew what he did, harm might come to them.

Since becoming single the last time, he swore that he had to tell Doc Johnson at least twice each month that he wasn't interested in trying matrimony again and to leave him the hell alone in the romance department. But it seemed as if Doc was a perpetual matchmaker when it came to his friend on Hog Plum Key.

Either because of weakness or strength of character, it was said that he let each of his two wives go and never chased after them to come back. No children, thank heavens, some in town opined, came of either marriage. After the second wife left, no one knew just how lonesome he was but no woman was ever spotted on the island again. At least, not until Doc Johnson got a call from his niece, Maggie Sullivan who said she would fill in at the clinic on a temporary basis. That's when things begin to change for the mystery man who lived on Hog Plum Key. It wasn't exactly what he had planned.

• • •

The Clinic. And so here I am, in a little town in the middle of the Everglades on the fringes of the Ten Thousand Islands, which I've since learned is, if you don't count the South Pole, undeniably the perfect place to lose yourself permanently or, if not permanently, at least for a long time. It's also, I've discovered, a place to meet some pretty scary, nefarious characters, none more mysterious than the man who lives on Hog Plum Key whom everyone calls "The Phantom" and in whom Doc seems to have a more than normal interest in having me meet. Of course, folks didn't call him that to his face. Most people never got a chance to talk to him face-to-face. Only Doc, Sheriff Billingsly, old Miss Jenkins at the store, and a few others ever got within a few feet of him. Most didn't want to. Most didn't know fact from fiction when it came to tales of the strange man who lived on Hog Plum Key. Surely no one would have believed the man, best known around here for soaking his feet in a bucket of bleach, had a law degree from New York University and, at one time, was invited to join a group of high-profile attorneys on Fifth Avenue.

The last thing I needed was to become involved with some back woods renegade who fancied himself a modern-day Robin Hood and I let Doc know that I had no intention of becoming involved with anyone, let alone a misfit who ran around the Everglades at night trying to get himself killed. I didn't care how noble he thought his cause.

Our first encounter took place exactly one week after I arrived in town. It was late and had been a busy day. Kids with runny noses, one snake bite victim and five people with food poisoning from eating Mae LaRue's egg salad at the Sunday church picnic had left both me and Doc exhausted but we needed to do inventory and send in an order for supplies from Ft. Myers early the next day. It was Tuesday, the day Lisa Reed came into my little cottage and cleaned and did my laundry. Thoughts of dropping exhausted into my bed with its fresh, straight-from-the-line sheets were scurrying through my brain, enticing me to hurry up and finish. I had just entered the last item on the long list when the door flew open and he charged through, all six foot, six inches of him. He took one look at me, grunted something unintelligible and walked over to Doc. Seems as if he'd surprised a group of men trying to steal his boat and, in the ensuing skirmish, a bullet had grazed his skull causing only a bit of skin damage.

"Lucky again," Doc said as he cleaned the superficial wound. "Damn lucky!"

Obviously Phantom Man was long on fights and short on words because when Doc said, "Meet my niece and nurse, Maggie" he just stared, mumbled something resembling "hello" and "thanks" and, before I could respond, he was out the door as quickly as he had come in. That was our introduction. And I thought all the nut cases were up North.

I had been in the Everglades for almost three months and was no longer surprised at his unannounced visits to the clinic and marveled that he seemed to get injured only after we had closed for the day. One evening, in particular, I thought would be his last. The wound ran clear across his throat and almost connected with the recently-healed scar that ended abruptly at his left ear. I think it might have been this night when I began to feel some crazy twinge of compassion for a person who obviously had a death wish.

"Sonofabitch!" he screamed as Doc pushed the needle through the torn flesh.

"No need to get testy, now," Doc said. "If you'd let me give you a little something to kill the pain..."

"No, damn it," he said. "Just get on with it."

"Nice road map of scars you've got," Doc said as he lifted the whiskey bottle off the shelf and poured a half glass of bourbon.

"Keep this up and pretty soon my handiwork will crisscross your face like the canals the developers had planned for the Glades."

Just the mention of how the Glades were almost lost to the greed of those who wanted to drain, farm, and develop her enraged the patient.

"Careful, old buddy," Doc said. "We got a lady present, you know."

He attempted a smile and grimaced. "Sorry, Ma'am, Sorry."

"No need to apologize," I said as I began to wipe away some dried blood.

Doc checked over the sewn-up wound again and offered to get his boat and take him home.

"Thanks," he said as he put on his shirt. "If the day ever comes that I can't drive my own boat back, Doc, you might as well get that autopsy table ready." And then, as was his habit, he was gone as quickly as he had arrived.

I just stared at Doc and ripped the bloody paper from the exam table. Doc was putting on his coat.

"You said he had two wives," I said sarcastically. "What happened to *them*?"

Doc grinned, turned and walked out on the porch. "Frog poop, my dear, frog poop."

I washed my hands, grabbed my sweater, turned off the lights, closed the door and followed him. Too tired to continue this conversation but too curious to let it drop, I leaned against the porch railing.

"What's that mean?" I asked. "What's the joke?"

"Well, Maggie," he said, turning and facing me. "There are a lot of things people can't abide in this here subtropical swamp. To some it's snakes; to some it's the ferocious mosquitoes and to some it's the threat of getting your house blown away by a hurricane."

"And...." I said. "To his wives?"

"Well, if the truth be known," he said laughing. "It wasn't the snakes, the bugs or the hurricanes that drove those two women away. It was that slimy, black frog poop they found every morning on the porch railing." He laughed and then added, "But only during the rainy season. Yup, that's what drove them away."

"Yuk," I said as I quickly pulled my hand away from the railing. "You're kidding, aren't you?"

"Nope," he said as he walked away. "But only during rainy season, my dear."

"Yuk," I said again, not quite knowing how to process this little bit of information.

"Ask him. He'll tell you, my dear. It was plain old Everglades frog poop that drove those two nice women away. That's all it was. Plain old slimy black frog poop. Ask him. He'll tell you."

Well, I can tell you right now that, even though I was beginning to admire someone risking his own life to stop the brazen and dangerous poachers who hunted in the Glades, I had no intention of asking him anything of the sort and I especially wasn't going to ask about his two ex-wives. But what I did decide is that it would be a cold day in you-know-where before I touched a porch railing ever again, especially during rainy season. Besides, the man had met me more than a couple of times in the clinic and had never done much more than grunt and cuss, with an occasional "yes" or "no, Ma'am" thrown in when I asked him a question. Yet, I had to admit there was this intrigue, more than just a little curiosity. What had made two women fall in love with him, enough in love to move to this remote wilderness? Perhaps there was more to him than just a self-proclaimed earth-protector with a death wish.

Several weeks later with lots of long nights at the clinic, I convinced myself that as soon as I mustered up the courage, I'd ask him to take me for a boat ride through the Islands, maybe take my new digital camera and snap a few shots of the bird rookeries that he spent his life protecting.

• • •

Back on Hog Plum Key, and once the whiskey took hold real good, he just wanted to sit back and soak his feet and listen to the swamp's chorus as it warmed up, soon to be in full swing as night descended over his island deep in the Everglades. Nothing satisfied him more than to watch the darkness rise up from the swamp across the little river as he heard the familiar sounds of the pig frogs, a far-away barred owl, the water lapping against the boat, and the soft wind moving through the tall Australian pines. He found himself thinking about Maggie Sullivan, her soft voice and the wholesome smell of her shampoo. He sensed a sadness about her but Doc had told him only that she'd had a rough year. Nothing more was volunteered and he didn't pry. Yet, he wondered what brought a beautiful nurse from the buzz of New York to a backwater town in Florida. Perhaps, one of these days, he'd ask her to visit some of the rookeries.

"Watch it, old buddy," he whispered to himself. "No time to be thinking that way." Yet no matter how he tried, his thoughts kept returning to Maggie Sullivan.

For a brief time, he almost forgot about the new gang of poachers who'd moved in from up north and the damn Wilkins brothers. Almost. Tonight he just wanted to exercise his bum arm and keep his feet from rotting off, which is what he told old Miss Jenkins was going to happen if she didn't soon replenish her stock of bleach. Seeing as how she didn't want to upset the man with the long red scar on his face who no one in town seemed to know much about, except that rumor had it that he was either a federal agent or a crazy hermit and that he'd killed for a lot less than a bottle or two of bleach, she promised to get a good supply in even if she had to go to Ft. Myers herself to bring it back. Of course, everyone knew that Miss Jenkins had never ventured outside of the town's limits by herself — and never would.

Tonight he was just alone with the full moon in early October, a week before deer season opened. He breathed in the smell of the wet flowers, the decaying leaves and the brackish and fresh water that all mingled together in the scent that he and every other animal knew so well. High overhead the sky grew dark and stars began to shine. A limpkin broke the night chorus with its wailing. He was filled with the sights and sounds of the Glades.

The last few days had been spent gathering firewood for the long, lonely cold nights that lay ahead. Two more days and he'd be able to forget the deer poachers and concentrate on those who wanted gators and plumes. Seemed like there was no lack of illegal prey to keep them busy. He welcomed just one night free from an encounter with the misfits who refused to obey the laws that protected the vast Everglades.

He leaned back in the rickety old chair and lifted the shotgun up and down; working his weak arm in the exercise that Doc told him he needed to do morning and night if he were ever to get any strength back in it.

Suddenly the air became still, the sounds of the limpkins and frogs quieted. Even the wind seemed to die. From somewhere not far away he heard the unmistakable baying of frantic dogs that told him they'd treed some poor critter that most likely had run hard and climbed high. It was blood they were after — a coon or a panther.

"Damn," he whispered. "It's them. The sonsofbitches are right here on my own place."

He kicked the bleach bucket aside and stood tall, listening to the sound of the crazed animals and the sound of a cornered panther, a sound that told him he had only a few minutes to cover a lot of ground, and barefoot at that, or a rifle bullet would rip into that beautiful beast and bring him down. For sure, he couldn't abide plume or gator poachers, but he got down right cantankerous when it came to dog hunters who'd just as soon shoot a helpless half-scared-to-death coon or panther, without even giving it a sporting chance.

He turned and ran into the dense woods. No time for shoes or extra shells. He cussed himself for leaving his revolver on the table after dinner. The loaded shotgun would have to do. He ran toward the swamp and the endangered animal.

He knew every inch of Hog Plum Key and could make his way from one end to the other with his eyes closed but, with feet tender from the eternal fungus and the night's soaking, every rock or shell he stepped on felt like a knife slashing his tender flesh. The moonlight helped him avert obstacles, but he was keenly aware that it also made him more visible to whoever had invaded his sanctuary. He moved fast but with great caution as the sound of the treed animal and the frantic dogs grew louder.

He crouched low when he came to the edge of the clearing. Two Black and Tans were frantically lunging at the base of the gumbo limbo and he could barely make out the figure of the panther high on an overhanging branch, teeth bared and eyes flaming in the dark. He had only a moment in which to decide whether to send the dogs scattering with a burst of shot or to lie in wait for the fast approaching men sloshing through the swamp from what he guessed was about a hundred yards in the other direction. One shot, two dogs or wait and maybe risk only getting one man. With a half-assed arm, he wasn't confident he could take on two. For a moment, he thought about Maggie Sullivan and wondered if maybe he should give it all up and try again for a normal life.

The crack of a twig behind him and to his right raised the hair on his neck. The smell of human sweat and stale tobacco told him it wasn't a wild pig or a raccoon. He turned just before something tore into his skull and sent him reeling to the ground. The last vision he had was a face he would never forget.

It was just before dawn when he awoke to the sounds of the island greeting a new day. A pileated woodpecker above him sounded like a jackhammer working on his brain. His head throbbed and his bad arm hung limp. Later he wouldn't remember how he managed to get to his skiff and guide it up the river to the city dock. Weak once again from exhaustion, hunger and loss of blood, he managed to repeat the half-walk, half-crawl to Doc Johnson's house.

● ● ●

I had spent the night tossing and turning, waking up, panicky, soaked with perspiration, failing to close down the kaleidoscope of shifting images that kept racing though my mind. But sleep wasn't going to come this night, not with alternating visions of the life I had left behind, that bastard Mark with his new love, and a crazy man who thought he was Tarzan of the Everglades. It was still dark outside so I grabbed a quick cup of tea and some cereal and left for the clinic. I had plenty to do and I didn't expect a patient before sunrise – but there he was.

Once again, I found myself cleaning his wounds while he slipped in and out of consciousness. I wondered what in the world would possess someone to intentionally confront death on a routine basis. A touch of alcohol to flesh startled him.

"Jesus," he said. "I thought Doc was brutal."

"Sorry, I didn't mean to be."

When I finished with the last of the stitches, he started to get up. I pushed him back onto the table and held one of his hands. Without giving a second thought to whom I was dealing with, I said with great authority, "You're not leaving here – not just yet."

I later learned that no one ever, except Doc, bossed this man around but that morning as he lay on the table, bruised and cut and aching, he looked at me with solemn blue eyes that seemed filled with pain and he gave me no argument. At that moment, I think I began to understand the man whose wounds I had tended countless times and about whom I knew so very little and, for some strange reason, I feared that our brief relationship had suddenly shifted onto a new plane. He lay back on the table, sighed and closed his eyes.

"Good," I said. "Now let's talk while we wait for Doc."

The slightest grin appeared at the corners of his mouth.

"What about?" he asked.

"What about what?" I said.

"Talk," he mumbled. "What do you want to talk about?"

I pulled a chair close to the table, sat down and said, "Tell me about Hog Plum Key. What's so special about it?"

He opened one eye and the grin turned to a full-fledged smile and for a moment I thought he might get up and leave. Instead he took both of my hands in his and closed his eye again. For a man whose vocabulary seemed to be limited to grunts and monosyllabic three or four word sentences, I couldn't believe what I was hearing. Descriptions of animals and the land and the plants came gushing forth as if he had been waiting a lifetime for someone to listen. I sat silently as he spoke about what had lured his parents to the area and what it was that brought him back. However, nothing touched me as much as when this towering man began to describe the orchids that could be found deep in the Everglades.

"On the trees, especially the buttonwoods, are orchids and air plants more beautiful than anything you might see in a florist shop on Fifth Avenue. There are butterfly orchids, mule-ear orchids, cowhorn orchids and night-smelling orchids."

"Is that all?" I asked.

He didn't bother to answer. Instead, he reached up and put his fingers on the back of my neck and pulled me toward him. I allowed him to touch my mouth with his.

I thought that this couldn't be happening but I didn't offer any resistance and whatever it was that had developed, unspoken until now, pulled deep at that very moment as we tasted each other. When he finally left the clinic later that morning, I knew that my life was changed forever.

• • •

On the ride back to Hog Plum Key, he couldn't get his mind off Maggie Sullivan and the sweet taste of her. He muttered to himself that he couldn't believe that he had just reached up and pulled her to him, had actually kissed her and that she had actually returned his kiss. Well, whatever it was, he'd deal with it later; maybe even ask her if she would like to take a ride through the islands. But, for now, he had just one more bit of work to do.

During the next few weeks, rumors raced through the town like wildfire when he hadn't been seen sitting on his porch soaking his feet. Most assumed that surely he had been killed or had taken off. Only when he finally showed up at the general store to pick up supplies, head covered by a stocking cap and one lame arm, did folks begin to connect him with the disappearance two weeks earlier of the Wilkins brothers and their two prized Black and Tan hounds. Those two dogs had cost over a thousand dollars apiece and had been ordered from a breeder in St. Louis. Most wanted to ask but, as usual, were too afraid to pry.

Months later, most also wanted to ask if there was any truth to the rumor that Doc Johnson's new nurse had been seen sitting on the porch at Hog Plum Key. They also wondered why Miss Jenkins latest supply of bleach arrived accompanied by a large supply of diapers.

• • •

I guess I won't be returning to New York or Washington any time soon. It seems as if the dreams — or nightmares — about Mark are a thing of the past. I kind of like this little town, with its down-to-earth people, even the ones who show up in the clinic with a backside full of buckshot and a don't-ask-any-questions look on their faces. As for the large supply of diapers that Miss Jenkins now has in the general store, only Doc and old Sheriff Billingsly and my mystery man and I know the truth and we're not talking.

And, as for the frog poop, it's true. Those little critters can poop a heap of black slime and any stair railing is fair game. But, hey, it's only poop and if you don't put your hands in it, it's no big deal. Anyway, the next big downpour will whisk it all away and there's always the dry season around the corner. That's the way it is with frog poop in the Everglades.

GUIDE FOR HIRE

It was early June and it was going to be hot. Real hot! Captain Johnny Shannon smiled as he thought of his old friend Cliff who once told him you know it's hot when the sweat runs down your back and uses the crack of your ass for a gutter. That's how hot it would be today.

Early morning was Johnny Shannon's favorite time of the day. At six o'clock in the morning in the small fishing village on the Southwest tip of Florida, not even the birds were awake yet. Soon the pelicans would arrive to take up their stations a few feet from the dock, bobbing patiently, awaiting a free handout. Shannon was soothed as he prepared for his charter by the soft slapping of the water as it met the bulkhead and the occasional drone of a motor boat moving slowly through the narrow channel into the Ten Thousand Islands and out to the Gulf of Mexico.

Five years earlier he closed the door to his criminal law practice at Rockefeller Center and said good-bye forever to the city he loved and the ruthless clients he hated and still feared. Defense lawyer Johnny Shannon headed to the Everglades to begin a life as a fishing guide and hoped that none of the cons he'd failed to get off came looking for him. The only law enforcement he cared about now was the local sheriff, who patrolled the waterfront for those who wanted to pick up a nice boat motor for free, and his nephew, Vance Johnson, back in D.C. Against Shannon's strong protests, Vance had chosen the Secret Service in which to work. No amount of pleading with the boy could deter him from his goal of landing on the President's personal detail. He was as determined as anyone Shannon had ever met and he eventually reached his goal. Now uncle and nephew communicated often, especially when Vance learned of the release of someone his uncle had reason to fear.

Unfortunately, Shannon hadn't been able to leave everything behind; he still possessed a keen ability to see right through most people and he trusted his intuition which last night signaled alarm as soon as he heard the phony Hispanic accent.

Shannon unlatched the door to the storage area beneath the console and checked the leather case. This was the first time in five years he had taken the Sig Sauer on the boat.

He walked to the front of the twenty-one foot Maverick and lifted the hatch where he kept ice and cold drinks. Satisfied that he had ample supplies for the day, he returned to his chair and leaned back and waited, thinking about what lay ahead. Every time he had a charter, he wondered if someone was coming to settle the score.

The sun, now a huge orange ball moving silently upward, cast long rays through the already-building thunderheads. June, beginning of hurricane season and an early tropical depression developing off the coast of Cuba, too far away to be a threat now, but one to be watched. He glanced upward. Would the storms wait until he returned to the dock? He stood quickly and walked to the compartment where he stowed rain gear.

The caller said he and his friend were in a hurry and wanted to book a trip far into the back-country of the Everglades National Park. Johnny had explained, as diplomatically as he knew how, that you had to be crazy to go into the back-country at this time of year; the bugs and the heat were just too oppressive. The caller identified himself as Anibal Colon. "We *want* to go to the back-country and I pay cash."

Some tax-free income this time of year couldn't hurt, so he agreed. What with the spring guiding season over and the summertime struggle for economic survival in full swing, a little sweat and a few bugs were the least of his worries. *Amateurs again*, he thought. Another day probably spent extricating expensive lures from entanglement in the mangroves. But, hell, a booking was a booking and what did he care if they were as dumb as a post.

He sat back in the Captain's seat, took a slug of hot coffee and relaxed for a moment as he thought about what lay ahead. Were the men really from Miami? Was there more to it than just a couple of guys seeking a day of fishing?

He looked at the sky again. Would the thunderstorm wait until he returned to the dock? More importantly, would he return to the dock?

He was ready. Mosquitoes and nosee'ms worked on him as he applied sun block and bug spray. He thought of all the questions they would ask. They always did:

"How do you know where the fish are?"

"What time will we come back?"

"Is it always this buggy?"

"Will we catch a big snook?"

His replies, always the same: "I don't know, but I have a good idea. About three-thirty. Yes, and maybe."

Shannon was a man of infinite patience and humor who tried never to let a client know when he had tired of their questions, the frequency of which directly correlated to the amount of beer consumed. Kids could be especially challenging; some a delight, others an absolute horror. He cringed as he recalled the twelve-year old, know-it-all from Philadelphia who for about the fifteenth time landed his lure in the mangroves and who, when warned against trying to pull it out by himself, did just that. Shannon could still remember the pain as the lure came ripping from the limb and into his cheek. The kid actually thought it was funny. He didn't think it was so funny when Shannon reached over and tipped him with one hand, grabbed both of his ankles and held him over the side while a large gator swam towards the boat. *Amazing,* Shannon thought, *how juvenile humor can quickly be displaced by sheer terror. Equally amazing,* he recalled, *the kid's father, instead of being mad that he had scared the living shit out of his precious offspring, later whispered in Shannon's ear as he placed a fifty in his hand,* "Thanks Captain, I gotta feeling he'll jump to the next time someone tells him to do something."

Shannon was a muscular man. His ruddy complexion from the sun and hands rough from cleaning fish and unkind hooks were evidence of the profession he had chosen. His six-feet, two-inch and two-hundred, sixty-five pound frame immediately made clients feel good about the guide they hired.

Yes, he loved this time of day when he had a charter. The evening before he studied the tide charts and weather reports, mapping out in his mind the route and fishing pattern he would take. Happy to have no distractions, happy to be getting on the water again and especially happy to be making a buck. Captain Johnny Shannon was definitely in his element. Except, this morning, he couldn't shake the feeling of unease. His guard was up.

He glanced in the compartment below the console to see if he had remembered his mosquito netting. One for the Captain. None for dumb customers who didn't know better. He walked back to the car to get the rest of the supplies he needed.

The town was nearly deserted, the oppressive heat having driven most of the winter residents north for the summer. Lights were just beginning to appear in the cottages of the few who stayed behind year round to battle the humidity, heat and bugs. Tour buses loaded with vacationers, mostly Europeans, would arrive shortly after sun-up, eager to experience the magic of Shannon's beloved Everglades.

Shannon locked the car and stepped back onto the boat to wait. The tide was up; a good time to leave. Damn fools better be on time, he thought. A no-show would really piss him off because he had given up his plan to spend the early morning pruning his hibiscus hedge. But a booking is a booking and his gut told him that this was one he needed to do.

• • •

Three blocks away Val Perez and Anibal Colon sat in the dining room of the famous Angler's Inn, its only customers. Perez, mocha skin, pudgy face with dark bags under his eyes, rheumy from drink and lack of sleep, and fifty pounds overweight, ran his fat fingers through his hair. With thumb and forefinger, he stroked the dark stubble that had erupted on his face overnight.

"Should've shaved, man, should've shaved."

Colon, tall, skinny, with a face deeply pocked from years of picking the acne scabs surrounding his crooked nose, a testament to many fights, and with straight greasy hair hanging across his eyes, was busy using a piece of toast to chase the remaining bit of fried egg across his plate.

"Nah," he said. "Don't want to look too clean. Remember, we're on vacation. Just a couple of guys ..." His words became muddled as the toast won the battle and he stuffed it and the egg into his mouth.

"Jesus Christ!" Perez said. "Why the hell did we have to get up before the fucking birds? What time we supposed to be there?"

"Seven, and stop your goddamn grousin', would you. We got time to finish the grub and go back to the room, take a dump and get the bag. He ain't goin' nowhere without us. Don't worry."

"What if he asks what's in the bag?"

"He ain't gonna. Now stop your goddamn worryin' and eat. Jesus! You act like a freakin' woman."

• • •

Silhouettes of the shoreline appeared quickly as the sun rose. Shannon sighed with relief as he watched the late model black SUV approach the dock and slow to a stop opposite the boat.

"Yo! You Captain Shannon?" the driver yelled.

Shannon nodded and motioned where to park the SUV.

The two men jumped out and opened the back doors. One grabbed a small cooler and the other a twelve pack of Corona. As they approached the boat, Shannon couldn't help but smile as he took in their clothing. Dressed alike, they both wore what looked to be new deck shoes, khaki shorts topped by Guayabera shirts.

Novices, Shannon thought. *Perhaps they are just a couple of guys out for a good day on the water.*

Anibal introduced himself. Val mumbled something and stuck out a hand.

While Shannon stowed the beer and the cooler, Val walked back to the SUV and returned dragging a large olive-colored duffel bag. Shannon watched as the two struggled to lift it onto the boat. He was curious but asked no questions. As a defense attorney, all he did was ask questions; as a fishing guide, he knew to keep his curiosity to himself.

"Let's get going," he said as the two men squeezed into the pedestal seats in the front, sat back and used the bag as a footrest. He brought the engine to life, untied the mooring lines and idled to the mouth of the river, gliding as effortlessly as the alligators who inhabited Florida's waterways and who, along with the pelicans, would be waiting for him later in the day when he cleaned the fish.

Dawn finally gave way to daylight. The cry of a red-shouldered hawk, followed quickly by the shrieking of a pileated woodpecker, interrupted Shannon's thoughts. He listened as the two men chattered away in Spanish. He understood just enough to know they weren't talking about fishing. It was now seven-fifteen.

"Hold on," Shannon yelled as he throttled to get the boat on plane.

"Holy shit," Val said over his shoulder. "How fast this thing go?"

"Only thirty," Shannon yelled. "But it feels like more." He pushed the throttle farther and the 150 horses gave a reassuring roar as he reached his running speed. Shannon was now completely on his own — cell phones and marine radio would be of little use where they were headed — and unless one of the Park rangers happened by to check his boat, they wouldn't see civilization again until he returned late that afternoon. The Rangers never bothered him. Other guides pissed and moaned every time they got stopped. To Shannon a Ranger stop was little more than a pimple on the ass of life and if you didn't cheat, you didn't have to worry. His motto was: *Take your time and be patient. If the fish didn't cooperate in one spot, they would in another.* Today he thought that a visit by a Park Ranger might not be a nuisance at all.

Before they crossed the Bay on the way to Sand Fly Pass and the Gulf of Mexico, Anibal and Val were already sipping their first breakfast beer — feet still firmly planted on the swollen bag.

Shannon guided the boat south through the maze of barrier islands and across the mouths of the Houston and Chatham Rivers, past mangrove islands with names like Rabbit, Pavilion, Mormon, Buzzard and Hog Key. Brown pelicans and osprey and ibis and a mud plume from an occasional manatee usually delighted his clients; only this morning, these clients seemed totally oblivious to anything but their own conversation.

The Glades was outlaw country, at times full of renegades and moon-shiners who roamed its vast waters, a haven for the lawless, but to Shannon it was a paradise of exotic vegetation, wildlife and birds like no other place on earth. However, he liked nothing better than to entertain his clients with jokes and tales of the nefarious characters who lived here.

Twenty miles south of town the water and the sky merged into one glaring, brilliant landscape. The boat made the wide turn into Lostman's River and headed east into the sun, through and up into the back country. Anibal and Val were now quiet and seemed uneasy as they looked around the unfamiliar terrain.

Shannon stopped the boat and suggested they try a favorite fishing hole and, although it was evident that both Anibal and Val knew the basic art of impaling a shrimp on a hook, their indifference and lack of enthusiasm for the sport of fishing was apparent. Shannon had fished these waters for thirty years and he knew when people were not really interested in what they were doing. Too many kids bored after the first hour, too many girl friends and wives who just came along to please someone else. It always showed through. These guys had about as much enthusiasm as a bowl of cold vegetable soup. He was glad he had the Sig Sauer aboard.

He tried several more fishing holes and was now in Indian Camp Creek, a narrow mangrove-lined waterway where a falling tide and shallow rock bottom could cause big trouble. Shannon raised the motor and guided the boat cautiously. Anibal looked over his shoulder with a painful expression.

"Captain, I have to take a shit!"

Shannon nodded and eased the boat to a small opening along the shoreline which led out onto the saw grass prairie. He nosed up onto the shore and tied off. Suddenly the mood turned more serious. As he started to step over the side, Val put his arm up and said "You wait here!" Shannon sat down and watched as the two men, both perspiring heavily, bent down. Both grabbed an end of the big bag, grunted and hoisted it up and over the side of the boat and onto the creek bank. It landed with a thud. Without explanation, they crawled over the side and lugged the bag into the marsh, cursing as they went.

As soon as they were out of sight, Shannon took the gun from its case and put it in an inside pocket of his jacket. He wondered just how ugly things were going to get. Except for the constant drone of insects, the Everglades had suddenly become silent and threatening.

Almost as soon as he had zipped the jacket, a loud piercing banshee wail penetrated the silence. Val and

Anibal ran from the marsh. The bag was gone. Both were covered with mud and their new clothes shredded by the teeth of the saw grass. Blood trickled down Val's arms and Anibal's shirt had a large tear on one sleeve.

"What the hell was that?" Anibal asked as he tried to climb back onto the boat.

Shannon laughed as both men slipped in the mud.

Val apparently didn't see any humor in the situation.

"It's not funny, Captain," he said. "We could have died in there with whatever that thing was that just screamed."

"Just a limpkin, boys, a harmless bird." He cupped his hands to his mouth and made the sound of the limpkin's cry: *Kree-ow. Kra-ow. Kree-ow. Kra-owgua.*

Val's eyes narrowed. "Enough with the fucking bird sounds. OK ? We go home now, Captain Johnny. OK!"

Shannon nodded, untied the boat and eased from the bank, retreating down the creek. The enormous white cottony clouds that decorated the endless clear blue sky only an hour earlier had suddenly begun to darken. The last thing Shannon wanted to do was spend the afternoon with these two in the shelter of the mangroves waiting for a monster thunderhead to pass.

It just might be closer than it looks, he thought. Racing a summer storm in open waters is always risky business but it's especially hazardous in Florida, the lightning capital of the world, but Shannon decided to chance it even though he could still remember clearly what happened a couple of weeks earlier when he lost a race with a fast-moving storm.

Kevin Brandon, an old friend, and his three sons had booked Shannon for two days in celebration of the oldest boy's 16th birthday. Kevin and the kids had been fishing with Shannon for four years and the Captain was their real-life hero. Halfway back to town, Shannon knew that he wouldn't be able to outrun the storm which was already pummeling them with hard-driving rain and pounding the flats boat on three to four foot waves. Near Possum Key, he sought shelter in a shallow mangrove-lined channel.

The storm — one of the most dangerous Shannon had ever seen — lasted over two hours with lightning so relentless it struck continually, appearing to slam the water on all four sides of the boat, often so close Shannon could see the fireball of each strike on the surface of the water. Kevin and the boys lay face down — too scared to move — while Shannon hunched down behind the console all too aware of the deadliness of a lightning strike in the marsh.

After the storm passed, Eddie and Steve were still trembling, eyes red from crying. Shannon had hugged them both and told them not to be ashamed, that he too had been scared enough to cry. "Heck," he said, "I almost wet myself." That night Kevin and Shannon sat on the dock drinking gin and tonic, happy to have survived one of the most dangerous weapons the Glades had in its arsenal.

● ● ●

Shannon throttled the engine, jolting both of his snoozing passengers awake.

"What the shit?" Val yelled over the engine's roar. Johnny motioned toward the dark sky and Val gave him an OK sign.

"Asshole," Shannon whispered to himself. *Might as well have some fun,* he thought as he took the curves around the mangroves just close enough to miss the overhanging branches. White ibis and snowy egrets erupted from the trees and around almost every turn an alligator submerged quickly.

Neither of the men spoke and Shannon welcomed the silence. He couldn't tell if they had fallen asleep but he was glad he had asked them to sit in the front of the boat on the ride back. He wanted them where he could see them.

By the time the boat eased up to the dock, it was late afternoon, golden with slanty sunlight.

Once they were all out of the boat and Shannon had tied her off, both Val and Anibal walked to their car, opened the door and reached in for something. Shannon followed.

Here it comes, he thought but then figured if they were going to do anything to him they would have done it already.

Val said, "Johnny, I pay you now." He reached into his pocket, pulled out a wallet and began to count out one hundred dollar bills — twelve in all. He handed Shannon the money and reached over and placed both meaty hands on Shannon's shoulders.

"The tab is only three hundred, fellas," Shannon said.

Val didn't blink as he got close enough for Shannon to smell his beer breath.

"Captain Johnny, we had a really great day. Consider it a big tip — a really big tip for forgetting about this day which didn't happen, did it?"

All of a sudden Shannon felt like he was back in New York dealing with the scum of the earth. He didn't need time to think about the right answer.

"You got that right, Val," he said. "I enjoyed my day pruning my hibiscus hedge."

Anibal laughed. "We knew you was a smart man, Captain, the minute we laid eyes on you."

As they walked back to the SUV, Val looked over his shoulder. "I wouldn't go back up that creek if I was you, Captain. That damn saw grass is some mean shit. If you ain't careful, it'll rip your nuts to shreds."

Shannon laughed and waved as they pulled away from the curb. "Didn't like that fishing spot at all, gents", he said.

Two days later, word spread like wildfire around the island. Two federal agents were in town talking to the local guides. It was no surprise when the black sedan with the government tags stopped in front of his cottage. He wished he had had a charter instead of taking the day off to tend his hedge, but he knew the drill; they'd wait around 'til he got back. Feds weren't welcome in town and most folks got real silent when strangers asked questions, especially questions from Feds.

"Captain Shannon?"

"That's me," he said. "What can I do for you fellows?"

They flashed their ID's in unison. One spoke: "I'm Agent Curran and this is Agent Jenson. We're out of the Miami office."

FBI agents, my ass, he thought. He'd had a lot of experience with Feds back in New York; he could smell a phony a mile away.

"Any unusual customers the last few weeks?"

He laughed. "All of my customers are unusual, some more than usual. Who are you looking for?"

Curran said: "Couple of Cubans looking for a place to drop some hot cargo."

"What kind of cargo?" Johnny asked, knowing they wouldn't tell him.

"Can't say, but it's imperative we find it."

Shannon stopped pruning and wiped the sweat off his brow. "Wish I could help you. I did have a couple of Hispanics, maybe Cubans, the other day — real duds in the fishing department, kept losing my good lures in the mangroves, caught a few fish, downed more beer than most, got sunburn and fed a lot of mosquitoes."

"Any chance they dropped anything off while you had them out?"

"Not a chance," he said.

Curran moved a little closer. "Nice hibiscus. Captain, are you sure?"

"About my hibiscus," he said. "Or about the Cubans?"

"You know what I mean."

"Sure, I do, but I'm afraid I can't help you. They were just a couple of city boys wanting to catch a few fish. I doubt they'll be back."

"Why do you say that?" Jenson asked.

"I can usually tell when novices get hooked on fishing — no pun intended." Neither agent laughed.

"They didn't act like it was something they would try again."

"Why don't you think so?" asked Curran.

"Too buggy, too hot, and my boat isn't the Queen Elizabeth. I think these guys expected something a little more comfortable."

"Any chance they paid by check?" Jenson asked. Shannon knew that the two men already knew the answer.

"Nope," he said. "Paid in cash. Three hundred plus a twenty tip. Kind of cheap but it was great entertainment."

"What's the usual tab?"

"Two-fifty or three, depending on how long they want to stay out. For these guys, three hundred worked just fine."

Shannon told them about the return trip, that he had dropped the two men off at the dock and that he hadn't seen or heard from them again. Curran and Jenson each handed him a card, thanked him and left.

Shannon watched the sedan slowly move down Waterview Drive and cross the bridge leading out of town. When they were out of sight, he made a quick call to Vance in D.C. and confirmed that there were no FBI agents named Curran or Jenson stationed in Miami.

"Thanks, Vance," he said. "When are you gonna bring the big boss down to fish with me?" They both knew this wasn't going to happen but they had fun with it anyway.

Vance laughed. "It looks like it's going to have to wait now 'til after election. Things are heating up pretty quick and with the situation in Middle East, who knows when he'll be able to get away."

"Thanks, kid, and take care of yourself." Shannon said and he hung up thinking what a freaking zoo it would be in town if a zillion Feds showed up all at once. There hadn't been a President here since Nixon was vacationing and fell off a fishing boat — not once, but twice. The newspapers had a field day with that one.

Shannon changed clothes and retrieved the Sig Sauer. He had plenty of time to get to the island and back before dark.

In the main channel, he turned to make sure he wasn't being followed. He had no trouble finding the place again and when he got close, he idled the boat and eased her up to the bank. He threw the anchor down and jumped over the side. About two hundred yards in, he found the bag at the base of a large cabbage palm. It was neatly folded and very empty.

Two weeks later, Captain Shannon picked up his mail at the Post Office. Among the bills and advertisements was a small white envelope addressed to "Captin Johnny Shannon". At least the name was spelled right, he thought. The envelope was postmarked Hoboken, New Jersey. There was no return address. He walked across the street to the city park and sat down on a bench. Inside the envelope was a small piece of white paper. The message was clear:

Captin Johnny, you done good. Me and Val had a good time fishing with you. We might want to come back. Take care of yourself. Anibal.

Shannon wadded the paper and the envelope and tossed it into the trash bin, confident that for some reason, he'd passed a test and that somehow, some day, he might again hear from Anibal and Val or the two men who supposedly were looking for them. But for now, big thunderheads were forming in the east and he had flowers to tend to.

RUN, RUN, RUN ...
AS FAST AS YOU CAN!

It is six o'clock on a warm winter evening in the small fishing village of Buttonwood, Florida, and the returning crab boats are jockeying for position in the narrow channel and the sun, full of golden orange, begins its rapid fall off the edge of the earth.

Every evening after the dinner dishes and homework are done, Eddie Reeser comes to this spot on the dock to cry and to think. It has been his favorite place since he first found it that hot humid day in May seven months ago, the day after he and his mother had driven into town with all their possessions tightly packed into the 24-foot rented trailer that she towed the eleven hundred miles from Maryland. It was at this place that he was at last able to find some relief from the sound of that one never-to-be-forgotten piercing shot, the siren at first far away and then closer and closer until it was so loud he had to hold his hands over his ears, and the image of the brownish red spot on the golden oak floor of his parents' bedroom, a stain that refused to give in to his mother's frantic scrubbings. The sounds and images in his mind and the spot on the floor were daily reminders that his mother was now a widow and he was fatherless.

"I won't live here with that spot!" his mother had screamed into the phone the night before she made her decision to move far away. That and the times he had overheard her muffled protests behind their bedroom door were the only occasions he remembered when her voice wasn't soft and gentle. He remembered how, as a little boy, he stuffed the bed sheet into his mouth to keep the sound of his own crying from being heard; a sound that he knew might bring swift punishment from his father. But that was only on the nights when his father came home late with the smell of alcohol on his breath and the sleepy look in his red-veined eyes. He only wanted to remember the good times like when his father's voice was as soft as his mother's and not confrontational. The good times had become increasingly fewer.

All efforts to convince his mother to rip out the oak flooring had been in vain and soon Eddie and everyone else knew she would never heal as long as she stayed in the house.

After the move to Buttonwood, it wasn't long before Eddie memorized the names of most of the small town's fishing fleet. *DogPatch One, Sea Note, Lost Cause, Flat Broke,* and the one he liked best, *My Maryland.* Could it be, he wondered, that there was someone else here from back home. Maybe someday if he ever felt comfortable talking to people in Buttonwood he would ask. Not now though, not this soon. They might want to talk, to ask questions, and he was not ready. Yet, it would be nice to know that his mother wasn't the only one who had made a bad decision. Oh yeah, he wanted to say, a really bad and stupid decision but he had promised that he would help put the pain of the last two and one-half years behind them. Eddie loved his mother, especially her strong determination, and he didn't want to make it more difficult for her than it already was. He just believed that a move eleven-hundred miles away from the busy suburb of Northern Maryland where they had lived since before he was born, where he had been an A-B, well mostly B-Plus, student with lots of friends and where the high school always had the best football team in the whole metropolitan area, where he probably would always be too tall for football, and where those few inches would have almost guaranteed him a spot on the basketball team, to a God-forsaken (that's how Aunt Peg had referred to Buttonwood) place at the end of the earth, a place with one school, no hospital, no drug store and where kids his age spent most of their weekends fishing or just hanging out at the city park, was stupid and unfair. The closest mall, which meant the closest video-game store or movie, was at least forty miles away. "Stupid, stupid, stupid," he whispered.

He watched as the larger vessels led the parade with *My Maryland* out front, slicing a path through the channel from the Ten Thousand Islands into the main harbor, the smaller fishing boats one behind the other riding smoothly between the crabbers' silver wake. "Yeah," Eddie said softly, "Go *My Maryland.*"

He enjoyed the nightly return of the local fleet almost as much as he enjoyed watching the antics of the greeters of the fleet — the pelicans — who at the first sound of the returning boats abandoned their pilings and their awkward plunges into the water and as a group took up their silent floating positions at the base of Captain George's dock to await an evening meal of fish carcasses.

Captain George had the distinction, Eddie learned from an article he read in the four-page local weekly, of being the oldest fishing guide in the Everglades and now that a lot of government attention and money had been directed toward reversing the damage that had been done years before by development and drainage, the media frequently sought a quote from the crusty old sailor. In his wildest dreams Eddie couldn't imagine what would possess anyone to live in Buttonwood willingly and do the same thing every day, over and over again.

As he watched Captain George, he was full of fear that he might begin to like someone in this place. He had only agreed to tolerate it, get the best grades he could and maybe a scholarship and then be out of here. He just hoped his mother would get the pain out of her system and decide to leave before then. He didn't want to know anyone who might change his mind. No way in hell, he thought. No way.

Just as he had memorized the names of the crabbing boats, Eddie also was quick to memorize Captain George's evening routine. As soon as the nameless nineteen-foot flats boat was secured on the lift and raised to the level of the dock, Captain George began to methodically remove rods, tackle, nets, cooler, and two thick vinyl bags and load them into the back of the beat up old blue van. Eddie often wondered what the bags contained and he often imagined something sinister — maybe a gun or some illegal object. He had read a number of books that told about the poaching and smuggling that often occurred right in Buttonwood.

As soon as the van was loaded, the slow-moving Captain began to scrub the boat. Once it sparkled clean, he fueled it for the next day's run.

Eddie sat on the dock, with elbows resting on bent knees and hands cupped on the sides of his face, the position he always assumed so he could watch through the spaces between his fingers. To any casual observer, he was just a boy looking out over the water. No way was he going to engage in conversation with anyone.

Captain George, the lower half of his face masked by a full gray beard, eyes yellowed from years in the harsh southern sun and surrounded by uneven lines of deep wrinkles, was tying the heavy rope to the cleats on the dock. As he bent over, jackknife position, legs straight and rigid, Eddie thought of his Grandmother Elsie and the way she tended her garden after her knees got too weak to squat.

"Can tell the age of a man or a woman," she told Eddie one day when he was helping her weed, "by the way they stoop or bend." Eddie was sad when she died but his mother said that she was very old and that it was her time to die. But it wasn't his father's time to die, not like that. No, he could never forgive him.

While he tied the last loop of rope around the stern cleat, the Captain turned his head toward Eddie and waved. Eddie, caught off guard, hesitated and then raised his right arm in a polite response and quickly turned his attention back to the pelicans. He squinted at the remaining third of sun, brilliant and radiant as it was being pushed over the edge of the earth by fast approaching dusk. A mosquito picked that moment, the moment when Eddie most wanted to remain motionless and unobserved and pretend he was invincible, to strike ferociously on the back of his neck and when he could stand the bite no longer, he swatted it so hard that he wished he had taken a less painful action.

"Ouch! Damn!"

"Nasty little critters, aren't they?" came the deep voice to his right.

"Sure are, sir." Eddie waved back and quickly cupped his hands to his face again but not before he took note of massive, deeply tanned arms each decorated with a blue tattoo just below the elbow. It was too dark to see the tattoos clearly and Eddie made a mental note to look closer tomorrow. He had never wanted to get a tattoo even though they were the rage with everyone, even girls, in Maryland and Virginia; he guessed sailors had been getting them forever. He figured that his mother would probably half-kill him; maybe even scrub his skin as ferociously as she had the stain on the floor until his skin might crumble and fall right off his arm.

Captain George heard that the young boy and his mother had moved from up North because the husband had committed suicide in a drunken rage just weeks after announcing that he had a mistress. He too had lost a parent under tragic circumstances and understood the pain felt by the young boy who sat and watched every day, drawn into himself and hiding his face.

Being a private person with a few facts of his own life better left unknown, Captain George respected the boy's solitude and acknowledged him with an occasional wave and comment about the weather or the fishing. It soon became obvious to Eddie that the Captain wouldn't intrude and he began to feel comfortable enough to just sit and watch without concealing his face. A gentle camaraderie, void of much visible sign, began to seep into both the old man and the young boy.

Eddie was glad that he no longer cried every evening and although he was beginning to change his mind about the move being stupid and cruel, except when the mosquitoes assaulted him mercilessly, he still wasn't ready to call Buttonwood home. However, he told his mother that he was making peace with it even if only on a temporary basis.

"I don't expect you to stay here after high school, Eddie," she told him one evening while they were doing the dinner dishes. "I never did."

"Are you going to stay?" he asked.

She got that far off look in her eyes that was by now very familiar to Eddie. "I'm not sure but I doubt it." Then she would laugh and tease.

"Maybe I'll move to the town where you go to college."

"Fine, Mom, but remember I live in the dorm and you live at least three miles away.

"Agreed," she said, "Your choice." And that is the way they always left discussions of how long either of them would stay in Buttonwood. It was the same way she concluded the frequent conversation about his refusing to do something that would ease the discomfort imposed by what he called creatures of the swamp, especially mosquitoes.

"Very well," his mother always said. "Your choice but if you get bit enough, you'll spray."

Even when the wind-driven rain battered his face or the mosquitoes bombarded him relentlessly, she knew he believed if he stared out over the water long enough and if he could endure the cruel insects, the pain he felt inside would disappear.

Later he would look back and be glad the way she handled his unhappiness. But that wouldn't happen for years.

Now the sun had slipped down in the sky and Eddie counted to himself the seconds until it completely disappeared below the horizon.

He jumped when the deep voice startled him. "Nice sunset, isn't it?"

He had been so lost in his thoughts that he hadn't even heard the door to the van slam shut and the Captain approach.

"Mind if I join you, son?" he asked as he held out his hand for Eddie to shake.

"No, sir, not at all."

"Been watching you watching me for a long time now," the older man said. "And thought you might like to get a little exercise; that is, if it's alright with your Mom."

Eddie didn't know quite how to respond but, for the first time in seven months, he felt less alone than he had since they moved to town.

"What do you mean, sir?"

"Well, I figure you probably know my routine pretty good by now and I'm sure you've noticed that I'm not a young man any more and I sure could use a hand every once in awhile."

Eddie was flattered and wondered what his mother would think since she had told him to avoid the crabbers in town because they were too rough for a young boy to hang around. But Captain George wasn't a crabber; he was a fisherman and maybe he would just ask her and give it a try. He was getting kind of tired just sitting on the dock and maybe, just maybe, he'd find out what was in those two vinyl bags.

Eddie thought hard about what was happening inside his heart and his head.

The Captain let the silence alone for a few minutes while they watched the last of the fishing boats, running lights leading the way, straggle in from the Ten Thousand Islands.

"What say we go ask your Mom what she thinks?"

The two of them stood, letting the calm tropical breeze blow over them, letting a friendship take hold.

JACK BE NIMBLE, JACK BE DEAD!

Jack Kroopenpopper's eyes blurred as they tried to focus on the silhouettes moving rapidly on the boat ramp below his bedroom window. The glow of a cigarette intensified. For a moment one figure stood motionless, then turned and stared directly at the second story window of the dark old cracker house where the boy watched through a narrow slit between the curtains. In the dark of his room, Jack took a deep breath and let the curtains close. Had the man seen him?

He remembered clearly the first night he heard the voices. He had tried hard to convince himself that the noise might be old Mr. Boondiddle, drunk again, and out walking, calling to the alligators. "Poor old soul," Jack's mother said. "He's new in town and needs friends who won't make fun of him." Jack and his pals were afraid of the old man and ran in the other direction whenever they saw him.

"Besides," she said. "I don't want you making fun of anyone, no matter how strange they act."

Like most young boys, Jack didn't stop his playmates when he saw them taunt and call the old man "Boonie the Loonie" even though he felt real sorry for him. Who could have known that before Christmas a crazy old drunk would save his life?

Jack quickly learned that the boys in his new school were rough, quick-to-fight chips-off-the-blocks of their fathers and uncles and brothers who worked long, hard days fishing and crabbing and long, hard weekends drinking and fighting. Most of them were born in Buttonwood, a little town in the swamp of South Florida which Jack's mother now called a Godforsaken mosquito-infested, critter-ridden swamp after she found herself just inches from an old, crusty moss-covered seven-foot alligator that had taken up residence on the back deck next to her prized gardenia bushes. It was bad enough that she feared her gardenias weren't going to make it in the torrid south Florida heat and salt spray; she was now supposed to share them with an ugly creature that would just as soon have her for dinner.

Folks from across town said they could hear Mary Kroopenpopper but what they couldn't know was that she was shrieking from anger, not fright. The entire town would soon know that Mary Kroopenpopper tolerated no nonsense and knew no fear, especially when it came to her prized Jackson and Perkins plants. That gator never knew what hit him. The heavy old railroad maul that Mary found in an antique shop in Skagway last year before the family moved from Alaska to South Florida came crashing down on that old gator's head so fast he opened his mouth, hissed once at the petite figure standing in front of him, raised up on all fours, turned and then hurled himself onto the boat ramp and slithered into the water. No one has seen that gator since.

Tom Kroopenpopper wasn't too happy with his wife's bravery; however, after having lived twenty years with the feisty woman he first met in Dublin, he wasn't surprised and knew better than to admonish her for an act that could have cost her a limb or even her life.

Jack sat on the floor of his bedroom for what seemed like hours listening to the voices below. What if he had been seen? What then? Exhausted, he finally crawled to his bed, jumped between the sheets and pulled the blanket over his head. Sleep was difficult what with his fear and the noises on the ramp below. He eventually fell asleep but not before the thought occurred to him that if he needed to cry out for his parents in the middle of the night, they probably wouldn't hear him. Their bedroom was all the way on the other side of the big house. He scrunched further down into the bed and said his prayers — adding a few extra for good measure.

The next morning at breakfast, Jack wanted to tell his parents what had been happening on the boat ramp for the past three weeks but he changed his mind. What if they didn't believe him? What if telling them would somehow put them in danger? They might think that he was unhappy about leaving his friends in Skagway and was making it all up. Just like he had done when his teacher asked the class to tell what their parents did for a living, he made up a story about his father being a famous writer of mystery stories. When he had finished and had taken his seat, all the kids in the classroom, except Dean Sanders, all sons of fishermen and crabbers, laughed out loud. How could he admit that he didn't know what his father's job was, except that they moved around a lot, sometimes with just a few days to pack up and leave?

Perhaps it had been old Boondiddle after all, he thought. Perhaps the old man had found another old drunk to talk to and both of them were down there in the soft glow of light talking to alligators or who knows what.

The second week Jack opened the curtain just enough to watch the shadows moving swiftly below. The third week, on a Thursday night, he excused himself right after dinner and went to his room and waited. Shortly before eleven, after his parents were in bed and the lights in the house were out, the now familiar scene repeated itself. Hushed voices, shadows of people scurrying back and forth.

Still, he didn't tell his parents or anyone else. By then he was too afraid. After the second week, when he'd got a better look, he knew for sure that it wasn't old Boondiddle. He also knew for sure who the men were and he knew that they were up to no good.

The routine was always the same; several hours past dark and one small boat that he guessed to be about an eighteen-footer, sitting low in the water, motor silent, slipped slowly up to the ramp. Three men jumped out. At the top of the ramp another man in a black pickup, with its open tailgate facing the water, smoked and waited. Soon the boat grated against the concrete ramp and the four men quickly ran back and forth between boat and truck. Then the boat, with its silent motor, would slip back into the water and the truck would ease slowly up the ramp and onto the road leading out of town.

One day after school Jack and his new friend, Dean Sanders, sat behind the school talking about sports and games.

"Is there anyone in this whole town that you're afraid of, Dean?" Jack asked. "Anyone besides old Boondiddle?"

"Sure," Dean said. "Lots of people."

Jack was torn between a desire to share his long-kept secret and the fear of being found out. Had he been a witness to something so dangerous that somebody might get real angry if they knew some kid was watching? He thought only a moment about his mother and father and decided it was safer to keep his secret to himself. After all, he had only known Dean since the beginning of the school year and he learned from watching old reruns of *Miami Vice* that something real bad could happen to him and his family. He made a vow right then and there to share nothing with anyone except Scruff. Old Scruffie would never tell.

He leaned close and whispered. "Dean, who are you afraid of?"

Dean whispered back. "My dad says all kinds of bad things are coming into town, drugs and illegal people sneaking into the country.

"Gosh," Jack said. "How does he know?"

"He just does," Dean said. "And it's best not to ever talk about it, too, he said."

"I'm not talking about it ever again," Jack said. "Not ever again — to nobody."

And after that conversation with his friend Dean, he never again brought up the subject of drugs or illegal people with Dean or with anyone else and each day after school he hurried home and went straight to his room.

During the rest of the fall semester, as the days got shorter, Jack began to fear his walk home. By the time classes were over and soccer practice was finished, it was close to dark. He was having a hard time concentrating on his studies. The burden of the secret he kept had become a real torment.

It was mid-December, just before holiday vacation and Jack was hurrying home from school. It was Thursday and he had a plan. Tonight he would wait until his parents were asleep and then he would creep down the stairs, through the long hall and into the laundry room right below his own bedroom window. Tonight he would get a real close look. He would learn everything he could about the men and what they were unloading and then maybe he would have the courage to tell someone. Maybe the FBI or the other people in the Government who had control over people who came into the county illegally.

He was really hurrying now, almost running. He didn't see the man come out from behind the bushes until he was right in front of him. For a moment all he was aware of was white crabbing boots and the putrid sweet smell of alcohol and tobacco.

Jack jumped back and tried to maneuver around the man but the stranger was too quick and too strong. Before Jack could react, a cold hand grabbed his left arm and another hand grabbed him by his hair. Right then, just like on *Miami Vice*, Jack knew he was going to die.

"What do you want?" Jack asked with a trembling voice. "I haven't done anything to you."

"Not yet, you haven't, you little punk," the man said as he let Jack's arm fall and reached into his jacket pocket. As soon as Jack saw the knife and heard it snap open, he knew for sure he was in deep trouble.

"Let me go," he yelled as he struggled to free his hair from the man's grip.

"See this knife, little boy?" the man asked, his face so close that Jack almost gagged.

The man loosened his grip and said, "Talk and you'll feel this knife, kid, and so will your alligator-attacking momma and your good-for-nothing daddy." And then he disappeared into the darkness.

In his whole life, Jack had never been this scared. He ran home faster than he had ever run before, slammed the door, jumped the steps two and three at a time and locked himself in his room. He knew he had to do something. But, what?

Jack put his plan to save the family into action that night. After his parents were asleep, he walked quietly to the laundry room, stopping long enough in the kitchen to get the heavy maul that his mother used on the old gator. It would take all of his strength but he knew he could lift it high enough to clobber someone over the head if he had to.

He had only a few minutes to wait before he heard the familiar sound of waves lapping against the bulkhead. The curtains didn't quite reach the bottom of the window and Jack looked directly out onto the ramp. He couldn't believe his eyes when the boat slipped up quietly and the first man jumped out, followed close behind by two others. The hair on the back of Jack's neck bristled as he saw each face clearly. He recognized all three of them. Now he was positive his parents wouldn't believe him. No one would.

Soon the driver of the truck got out and walked down toward the others.

As he got just below Jack's bedroom window, he stopped, looked up and motioned. The three men from the boat looked up and nodded, then quickly began to unload the boat.

Jack's heart raced so fast he was sure it would jump right out of his chest and for a moment he couldn't catch his breath. Without waiting for the men to finish, he ran to his room, closed and locked the door. What could he do now? They knew.

He lay awake all night hearing every sound the old house made, sure that someone would bust down the door to silence him forever. Palm fronds brushed against the shutters. Was it someone climbing a ladder? Was it the raccoon that had a habit of sitting on a limb a few feet from his window? At last, he fell into a fitful sleep just before his mother woke him for school.

Feigning a stomach ache and sore throat, he convinced her that he was too sick to get up. She believed him because he was very seldom sick and loved school. She told him to stay under the covers and went downstairs to fix him a warm cup of tea. By the time she got back, Jack was sound asleep.

Jack slept on and off all day but when his father got home and came into the room, Jack was fully awake. He desperately wanted to tell his father what he had seen every Thursday night for weeks but each time he thought he had mustered up the courage, fear took over and he kept quiet.

At ten o'clock, Jack pretended to be asleep when his mother and father came into the room to see how he was and to turn out the light. Once again, Jack waited until he was sure they were safely asleep in their own bed. He wasn't sure what he was going to do, but he knew he had to do something.

Even in South Florida, it can turn cold during the winter and tonight the temperature was going to drop to thirty-eight degrees. He had heard the weather forecaster on Channel 7 warn of a freeze in the citrus groves.

He bundled up and let himself out into the cool night air. Scruffie tried to follow. "Stay back, old pal," he told the tabby who was rubbing against his legs. "Hush, cat, or you'll wake the whole house."

For what seemed like hours, Jack walked back and forth on the little street where his house stood, keeping out of the glow of the streetlights and trying desperately to decide what to do. Should he run away and never come back? Would that save his parents? He would miss them terribly and he was sure they would miss him. But wouldn't that be better than getting them killed? All because he was a nosy kid and had seen something he wasn't meant to see. He fought back the tears.

The faces of the three men flashed over and over in his mind and he could still feel the cold knife against his throat. No one would believe him against the word of these three men. No one! Not one soul would believe the new kid in town, a ten-year-old, against the word of three of the most influential men in town. He sat down on the dock and cried. It was hopeless.

Once again, he didn't hear the man step from the bushes. He smelled the putrid breath first but it was too late to run. There was no mistaking who had grabbed him from behind and what he felt pushing against his throat. Just as he started to scream, a gag was forced into his mouth.

"Ya little spy," the man in the white boots hissed. "I'll teach you something about snooping 'bout things that ain't no concern of yours." With his left arm around Jack's throat and his right hand holding the cold blade, the man moved backward toward the dock, dragging the struggling boy in front of him.

Jack was now praying with all his might, trying desperately to remember the special incantations his Irish mother had taught him and if there was a Saint he could call on for just such a situation. He began to whimper and felt the sting of tears on his cheeks.

"Shut up, ya little coward," the man said. Jack gagged and thought he would throw up. He was being dragged closer and closer to the water's edge; his eyes closed as if that might make the man disappear.

Without warning, something big and powerful sprang from the sea grapes and hurled itself at Jack's attacker. Jack felt the grip around his throat lessen and heard the cold knife hit the ground. He was thrown aside where he curled into a ball and covered his ears.

The struggle lasted only a moment. Jack heard a loud splash in the water and then there was only the sound of the palms swaying in the night, the croak of pig frogs and the sound of footsteps moving toward him. Jack shivered, too afraid to move. All of sudden, he remembered the prayer he had that had eluded him and in between sobs he said it over and over again:

O Lord, be between us and harm and protect us from the harm of the world.

O Lord, be between us and harm and protect us from the harm of the world.

The footsteps got closer and a figure leaned down close to where Jack lay.

O Lord, be between us...

A deep voice interrupted: "It's OK, son. You'll be OK now. Get up!"

Two strong arms lifted Jack to his feet and held him close until he stopped sobbing. Jack finally got up enough courage to look up — it wasn't the mean face of the crabber that he looked into but the face of Old Boondiddle. Jack started to speak. The man put his fingers on his lips. He wasn't drunk and he didn't speak crazy.

"Shhh!" he whispered.

"But, who...? What...?" Jack said.

Old Boondiddle leaned down. "Go home now, son, you'll be O.K."

What about my mom and dad?" Jack asked, still trembling as he tried to figure out what had happened.

"Go home, son," the man said firmly. "Your family will be fine and so will you."

"I don't understand."

"You're not supposed to understand, son. Just remember that this never happened, OK?"

By the time Jack could answer, Old Boondiddle, or whoever he was, had quietly slipped away into the dark of the night.

SILENT NIGHT

Silence. That terrifying, indescribable sound of silence that can paralyze, enveloped her like a soft fog on a winter morning. Ann Sayre knew he was in the house somewhere, looking for her, waiting for her to make a mistake, to let down her guard, to forget for one second that the threat was real, that he really would find her and finish her off, like he had all the others. The silence told her he was there, waiting. Would her hiding place — a virtual fortress in her own home — be enough?

Now fear invaded her, hunkered down deep inside her gut. As she sat listening to the sound of her own breathing, the realization that her life would never be the same crashed in on her and she wept silently. She had felt such pride when Jefferson County selected her as a juror. She would play a major role in the system which would, she hoped, bring Randolph Tucker, one of the most depraved criminals in the country, to justice. At first, uncertainties about her own objectivity caused her to consider disqualifying herself.

"Damn it, Carolyn," she told her close friend the night before the trial began. "What if we're all so objective, so scared that his attorney finds some tiny loophole and he walks?"

"Or ..." Carolyn said. "... some dumb bleeding heart on the jury buys an insanity plea and feels sorry for the monster and he's out after a year or so in a mental ward." The two friends looked at each other.

"He's not insane. He's evil!" Ann said.

Each thought the same; Tucker mustn't walk — ever! Ann Sayre would cut him no slack.

The lawyer's questions remained vivid.

"Ms. Sayre, do you have a problem with the death penalty ... ?"

"No, sir," she replied.

"Has anyone in your family been convicted of a serious crime or ..."

"No, sir."

The questions persisted, the lawyers challenged the way lawyers do and, at long last, a jury. Ann's wish had come true; she would not feel guilty of prejudgment and vowed to see Tucker get the death penalty. The prosecutor strolled slowly to the jury box and began his opening statement.

"Ladies and Gentlemen, it is your responsibility to determine the truth; to see that justice prevails ..."

Thank God, no one can read my mind, Ann thought. Never for a moment during the long tedious trial did she forget what Tucker had done; not for one minute did she doubt his guilt.

The prosecutor slowly turned and pointed to the defendant.

"The word *grisly* is inadequate to describe the manner in which this man, Randolph Tucker, snuffed out the lives of ten young people."

Ann looked directly at Tucker. Their eyes locked and she knew she was looking at raw evil.

The prosecutor turned toward the jurors.

"Ten young people who didn't have a chance died a horrific death."

The carnage had spanned five months; a lifetime in a community where some folks still didn't lock their doors and the most serious crime during the past ten years had been the hidden plot of marijuana the Sheriff discovered up on old Zeke Morris's farm. Five months of terror, an entire community held captive, citizens paralyzed with fear and disbelief, afraid to venture out alone even during daylight. Tucker had raped, murdered and dismembered nine women and one man. Guns brought down from the attic, children not permitted outside without an adult and relatives calling from everywhere begging family members to leave town. A monster was in their midst, someone who managed to enter and leave without so much as a trace of evidence and, scarier yet, a monster who appeared to have selected his victims with great thought. How? And why?

The prosecutor's voice rose. "Raped, murdered, dismembered. Nine young women and one young man." His words hung heavy like a wet snowfall in late winter.

Ann wasn't the only juror who knew all of the gory details. The media frenzy began the day the second body was found – the major networks hurled the story to the masses twenty-four hours a day. Ann figured they'd have to go to the far reaches of the universe to find anyone who hadn't read or heard of the case.

No fingerprints and no DNA – anywhere. Instead he left another calling card – the contorted remains of his victim, posed to shock. No one in town would ever forget that Deputy Sheriff Martin, the first to open the door at nineteen-year old Karen James' apartment, remained in therapy, unable to work, unable to escape the image of a severed head, eyes frozen open in fear, resting between her legs. There had been no signs of forced entry, no indication that any of the victims knew Tucker or would have let a stranger into her home. All had sophisticated security systems. The one thing that puzzled investigators — could it have been a coincidence? — each victim had a grandfather clock and in each case the pendulum stopped moments before the estimated time of death.

The public defender assigned to Tucker's case could offer little in the way of defense. Tucker's past was sketchy. His mother committed suicide when her son was ten and a grandmother and an uncle, now both dead, raised Tucker. Beyond this, there was little investigators could learn about Randolph Tucker. It was as if everything in his life after he turned twenty had been erased and if he hadn't confessed to the murders, there would be nothing to build a case on. Investigators weren't even positive who Randolph Tucker was.

According to state-ordered psychological evaluation, the defendant was mentally competent to stand trial. Ann wasn't sure she could understand how evil of this magnitude could classify as mentally competent. She was sure of only one thing: Randolph Tucker, or whoever he was, was evil and needed to be put away forever. Case closed!

Ann slumped against the wall, closed her eyes and let the memories of the five-month ordeal play out once again in her exhausted brain. She could see him clearly; short and wiry, baby face that looked pubescent, not yet affected by acne or facial hair, eyes dark and narrow hinting at the evil that lay beneath and when he stared directly at her, the hairs on the back of her neck bristled and gooseflesh erupted on her skin as if he could see deep into her soul. She shivered as she remembered the bailiff's veiled caution the second day of the trial – or was it sick humor – when he pulled her aside and whispered in her ear.

"You know, you're the only juror who fits the profile of his female victims."

"I don't need confirmation of an observation I made the minute the jury was seated, thank you." The bailiff smiled; her sarcasm seemed to amuse him.

Ann forced her mind to the present and glanced around her hiding place. Had she forgotten anything? Would it be enough? Satisfied that she had done all she could, she let her mind wander back to the courtroom.

The Judge bellowed into the silence:

"Randolph Tucker, you have been found guilty of ten counts of first degree murder ..."

A collective sigh rippled through the courtroom.

"Do you have anything to say before I pronounce sentence?"

The animal who had without compassion or mercy replaced the light of life with the dark of death as casually as one extinguishes a candle, stood erect, hands motionless at his side and slowly turned to face the jury. The dark eyes swept slowly from juror to juror, holding each one captive, delivering a special message of revenge, hate spilling slowly over his thin lips like thick Missouri molasses.

"I'll be back to visit ..."

He stared directly at Ann.

"... each of you."

The courtroom erupted with jeers. The Judge banged the gavel and roared, "Silence! Bailiff, remove the prisoner!"

The judge's words were a blur; Ann felt Tucker's stare burning into her. She wanted it to be over, to get out, and get away from it all. She left for California three days later to spend a few days with her parents. Instead she stayed two weeks, slept until noon each day, visited old friends, and in an effort to clear her mind, enjoyed long discussions with her mother on the patio overlooking the Pacific.

"Stay longer," her mother begged when Ann announced plans to leave for home. "Or at least let your father go back with you."

Ann refused, saying that she couldn't stay away forever. As her parents waited for her to board her flight, she hugged them like a reluctant child being sent off to summer camp.

"Thanks for everything," she said, trying to sound casual. "I'll be fine, honest."

Her father put his arm around her shoulder.

"Your mother and I are terribly worried about you. You've been through so much."

She whispered in his ear. "I love you two and I promise I'll call every other day." Then, as if to reassure herself, she said, "Remember, he's locked away for good or on the way to the gas chamber."

At the gate, she hugged them both again. "I love you. I promise I'll call often." A loud voice announced immediate boarding and Ann kissed her father on the cheek where a single tear hung suspended. She turned quickly and rushed toward her plane.

• • •

Ann and the townspeople set about their business and tried to forget, knowing they never would. Ann volunteered longer hours at the Thrift Shop. When she stayed busy, her mind resisted most of the horrible images that were etched within.

The bad news arrived with an abrupt phone call from Chief of Detectives Sam Jackson. Ann took a deep breath, afraid of what was coming. He wasted no time on formalities and got right to the point. When he told Ann that Randolph Tucker had escaped, she instantly felt her chest begin to constrict. She struggled to take in air.

"What! How the hell ... ?

"Faked a heart attack. Managed somehow to get out in a service truck," he said. "Not quite sure how he did it, but we are alerting everyone involved with the trial."

Ann slipped to the floor and gripped the phone. Her heart pounded and she could feel blood race through her veins. Not a day had gone by since the trial when she hadn't thought about Tucker's parting message to the jury. The stare. The threat. Suddenly the evil sprang to life and once again the images of the victims tormented her.

"Sorry to have to worry you but we'll get 'em."

The line went dead and fear flooded through her. She had never felt so alone or so scared. How much did Tucker really know about her? Jackson's parting words gave her no solace.

"So this is how I'm rewarded for doing my civic duty!" she screamed at the empty house.

Two days after his escape, Randolph Tucker made good on his promise and Ann's world began to crumble. Sandra Polston, juror number four, died first. No one saw her fall into the path of a speeding train. Next, William Callaway's throat was slit as he lay sleeping beside his bride of two weeks. Melinda Copeland — found strangled to death in her bathtub, her husband and three children watching a video in the family room a few yards away. It didn't take Tucker long to finish off every juror except Ann. Case by case the same. No witnesses, no fingerprints and no evidence. After the third juror died, the police provided security for the remaining jurors, protection that proved to be inadequate to save their lives.

The FBI stepped into the case and the search for Tucker became one of the most intensive in the country's history. Security around Ann's home and the Thrift Shop doubled and then tripled. She began to wonder if she would go crazy and at times imagined that one of her protectors was, in fact, Tucker in disguise. She lay awake at night and thought about where he could be and when he would make his move. She prayed that he was dead.

Months passed without incident and most of the town's residents began to fall back into their old routines except doors were locked and barricaded and the owner of "Superior Security Systems" reported a booming business in everything from deadbolts to full house security systems.

The small library of Jefferson County, under the watchful eye of the widow Claudia Parker, had only one small room, four square wooden tables, one copying machine, two windows and 400 books. The library shared space in the courthouse basement with the retired files of the county building inspector. Claudia Parker, or Miss Claudia as everyone in town called the quiet librarian, knew the exact location of every book in her inventory, who had checked out each volume and when it was due back. She amazed everyone with her ability to remember overdue fines and, for all her graciousness in greeting visitors to her domain, she had no compunction about reminding those in arrears whenever and wherever she encountered them.

Until several months before the murders, no one had expressed any interest in the old musty boxes filled with county building plans and so Miss Claudia was surprised when the dark-haired man with the thin black moustache, who introduced himself as Al Greeley, asked to see the old files. He told her he was gathering information for a book he was writing, a book that would be titled "After the Wars: Getting America Housed". Miss Claudia was eager to help and readily showed him the old files. She herself had been a war bride, sharing a tiny one-bedroom apartment with two other couples and four babies. She told him she knew firsthand how difficult it was to find housing back then. Months later, after the murders, she told detectives that Greeley had arrived at the library early in the morning and stayed until closing four days straight. He painstakingly examined and copied every building plan in the old files. She remembered that the stranger had begun his daily visits to the library in the months just prior to the murders.

• • •

Just when Ann began to believe that Tucker couldn't break through the constant blockade surrounding her and that her life might be spared, the cloak of FBI protection was suddenly ripped away and, once again, she felt naked panic. The call came early in the morning; The Bureau was sending Allen Smith, the Area Director, *personally* to talk to her. He would be there within the hour.

Ann sat on the front porch of her two-story suburban home waiting, nervous and agitated. She watched the activities on the lawn next door. A moving van had parked diagonally on the grass and three muscular young men darted back and forth like frantic ants, pushing and lugging furniture and boxes. The "SOLD" sticker had been placed on the "FOR SALE" sign the week before and Ann was glad that the house wouldn't be empty much longer. The Evans family, Paul and Jane and their two teenagers, had moved away shortly after the murders.

"Good friends, always," they had pledged when they sat together in her living room on the Evans's last night in Crompton Estates, pouring through photographs taken of two families who had survived PTA meetings and T-ball together. These were her dearest friends and they had been there for her as she grieved the untimely death of her twin sons in a school bus accident and then seven years later the unexpected death of her husband. It was Jane who had urged Ann to volunteer at the Thrift Shop.

SILENT NIGHT

A thin man dressed in faded jeans and plaid long-sleeved shirt leaned against the large crabapple tree watching the unloading operation. Ann wondered if he were the new owner. She thought the furniture cheap, like rental office furniture, pretty sparse for a family. *Perhaps he is a bachelor – obviously with little taste in decorating.*

Ann watched the procession next door until the shiny black sedan with government tags moved slowly around the corner and came to an abrupt halt in her driveway. The front passenger door opened and a tall man in a black suit with a starched white shirt and shiny black shoes stepped out. The driver stayed behind the wheel, the motor running. Ann glanced back toward the moving van next door. The man who had been leaning against the tree was gone.

Allen Smith was tall with thinning blond hair, bluish-grey eyes and a face that sent messages of sympathy and concern before he spoke. Ann guessed he had selected himself for this task because of some paramount importance the Bureau attached to whatever news he was to convey. He stood poised and professional in the foyer of her suburban 1950's two-story home. They exchanged pleasantries. Ann asked him to get right to the point. He did.

"We're sure that Randolph Tucker is dead or has fled the country or we wouldn't be suspending the surveillance." The word "suspending" catapulted her out of the cocoon of safety and into grim reality.

She was prepared for bad news but not for this. She sank down on the hall stairs and let the months of stress, hidden under the mantle of self-confidence, release.

Allen Smith was sorry. He told her there was nothing he could do. It wasn't in his hands. If it were, he wouldn't suspend and so on. The official line. That was it. Nothing could be done. She listened in disbelief as he told her that no amount of begging and pleading could change the fact that the area budget had been stretched to the limit and the decision was made at a higher level. Not even the criminal of the century could sway the powers in charge of budget and the budget had no dollars for further protection for Ann Sayre.

She thanked him. He pulled a business card from his suit pocket and told her to call if she needed anything. They shook hands and he walked quickly to the car and left. She was alone again. Terribly alone. She sat on the stairs and sobbed as the realization set in that only she could save herself. Later that night, as she lay awake listening to all the voices of a forty-year-old house, she began to devise a plan which eventually would consume her night and day until it was over. The FBI could believe he was dead if they wanted to, she thought, but without a body, she knew Randolph Tucker was alive and that he would come for her. It was just a matter of time. She remembered the eyes.

• • •

Now it was the point of no return, the space between life and death. Would all the planning work? In the silence of her small fortress she went over and over again the precautions she had taken. The room in which she sat alone and scared had recently been remodeled. The carpenter, carefully selected as much for his ability to be discreet as his ability to explicitly follow her design, and the man who had recommended him were the only ones who knew the reason for the unusual work he was hired to do. Co-workers at the Thrift Shop, family, and those neighbors who had taken note of the old faded blue van with *Marvin's Home Repairs* written in bold letters on the side, were told that Ann had been wanting to remodel her outdated bathroom for years, its termite-damaged wood finally to be replaced. Nothing out of the ordinary she told them, just a project to keep a woman busy who had lived through hell and was trying to get her life back. Believable? Perhaps.

She found Marvin Langley through Jack Blanchard, an old golfing buddy of her husband's. Jack had been with the National Security Agency, training agents in the art of surveillance and counter-surveillance. She hadn't seen or spoken to him since her husband's funeral. When she ducked into the Ace Grocery and borrowed the phone, she reached Jack on the first try. He had been following her case and was eager to help.

"If the police feel he has skipped or is dead, what makes you think differently?" he asked after Ann had explained.

"I just know," she said. "I watched his eyes during the trial. I listened to his threats. I'm the only one left ..." She hesitated, as if wondering whether to share the most compelling reason.

"My gut tells me that he isn't finished, he's just waiting and playing with me. It's like a game to him, he's the cat and I'm the mouse and he can finish me off anytime he wants. He knew the police would pull out sooner or later. He wants to see how I react. What I'm not sure of is how much time I have left before he pounces."

He told her about Marvin Langley.

"You can trust him with your life," he said.

"That's exactly what I'm doing."

Jack asked if he could do anything else.

"Thanks, Jack, now I just have to depend on Marvin.

"I promise you, Ann." Jack said. "You won't find anyone more capable or trustworthy than Langley. I doubt if even his wife knows that the Government provided most of his paycheck." Ann began to feel more confident. She listened intently as Jack gave her some background on Langley.

"Langley even carried a top secret clearance," he said. "Probably still does. If he hadn't decided to slow down, fish more and enjoy time visiting the grandbabies, he'd still be working for the Feds."

He hesitated and then asked. "What if I move in for a few months?"

She thanked him profusely and just as she had refused her father's offer to come and stay with her, she politely refused.

"I have to do this alone Jack," she said. "When he comes for me, it won't be when anyone else is around. He'll just wait. He has nothing but time and it will be in my house. I'm sure of it. It won't be at the train station or at the Thrift Shop. It will be right here."

As soon as the connection was broken she dialed Langley using the unlisted number Jack gave her. They agreed to meet at her house at ten the following morning. It was Wednesday – she hoped he could begin work soon.

Marvin Langley's hands were rough and callused and looked the size of baseball mitts, the hands of a man who had spent most of his life earning his living with them. His handshake was firm but not overpowering. Ann guessed his height at over six feet. Muscles strained the sleeves of his shirt. He had a friendly face and a head full of disheveled bright copper hair.

They sat at the dining room table, blinds completely closed, two sets of design plans laid out before them, one a fake that Ann instructed him to carry with him at all times; the other, she told him, he must follow explicitly and, when he wasn't actually using them, were to be left with her.

Ann handed him a note that explained the two sets of design instructions:

Anything we say here or any place in public could be overheard. This is the work I want done with complete instructions. No one – I mean no one besides you and me – is to know of the actual work you will do for me. In the house or in any place where we talk, refer only to the work outlined in the first set of instructions.

The note also contained the name and address of a decorator in the downtown area, a place she had picked randomly from the yellow pages. She asked him to meet her there the next morning. Then she would give him all the details.

He read the note, nodded, and handed it back to her, falling into his part without hesitation. "I can't believe how many people are remodeling their bathrooms these days," he said. Instantly, Ann felt better than she had in months — better although not quite safe. Hard as it was for her to believe, she knew that Tucker could already have bugged her house.

"I'll have an estimate drawn up by tomorrow morning," he said. " If agreeable, when do you want me to start?"

She smiled, pleased with Marvin Langley. He would begin work on Friday. They stood on the front porch and shook hands once again.

After he was gone, Ann went to the bathroom, took a pack of matches from her pocket and burned the note before flushing it down the toilet.

"One point for the mouse," she whispered.

The next morning, she arrived at the decorator's five minutes before her appointment with Marvin. She spoke with owner Sally Drugal who, sensing a substantial profit, readily agreed to lend an office where Ann and her carpenter could meet. When Marvin arrived, she introduced him to Sally and ushered him into the small office at the rear of the building.

"Jesus," he said when she had explained everything. "I know this case. _Everyone_ knows this case. I've seen some bad ones, but this guy takes the cake."

Marvin promised to begin work immediately and he did. He worked fast and took breaks only when Ann brought him something to eat or when he needed to use the bathroom. He had Ann's hiding place completed within five days and after she inspected it, she grabbed him around the neck, kissed his check and began to cry. Marvin knew he had done all he could do.

"I can stay longer, if you want," he told her.

"Oh, how I wish you could, but I know I have to do this myself," she said. "I know he won't show unless I'm alone and he thinks it's on his terms."

Marvin held her hands. "You'll lock down, won't you? The minute you suspect anything."

She assured him that she wasn't about to take any chances. Marvin gave her one last explanation of the two monitors and then he was gone. She had felt so safe while he was working on the room. Now she felt totally helpless. She had learned a great deal about Tucker and she felt certain he would reveal himself to her in some way before he struck. She would have time to hide while he enjoyed his next victim's fright. But how in the hell would he get in? How in the hell did he get in any of the other places?

• • •

Ann didn't have to wait long to use the "fortress." It was Sunday; four days after Marvin had completed the room. She awakened at five a.m., before sunrise, and moved the slats of the blinds just enough to peek at the street below. The telephone truck was back, its silhouette barely visible in the fringe of the glow laid down by the corner streetlight. She had seen it parked in front of Pam and Jim Johnson's several times after the room was finished. Strange, she thought, since the Johnson's were cruising the

Inner Passage in Alaska and not due to return for another week.

Something else alarmed Ann. The day before, Regina, the coordinator at the Thrift Shop, phoned to tell her that she had taken two calls for Ann but when she told the caller that Ann was off for several days, the caller hung up. If Ann hadn't such an intense, overwhelming intuition that told her it was time to hide, she might have thought herself paranoid. Tucker had waited to make sure Marvin wasn't coming back. He was playing with her. It was time to hide. Quickly!

A small lamp lit the room where she waited, invisible from outside. The room was totally isolated and secure with solid fireproof walls, roofing, flooring and a steel door that had been disguised upon delivery as the base of a modern pink six and a half foot tub. The gun, a 357 Magnum loaded with hollow points lay on the floor close to her. Her powerful cell phone also lay nearby. She looked at Allen Smith's business card and wondered how long it would take him to get to the house if she called.

Ann had left nothing to chance — nothing that she could think of. If he got through, and surely he couldn't, she had the gun. She had a few supplies — snacks, several bottles of water and the shoebox full of old letters that Marvin had found tucked away in the crawl space above the garage. The letters were postmarked in the 50's; the box tied with a faded pink ribbon. She would read a few while she waited.

A hidden generator powered the elaborate monitor with its many blinking red lights — one for each entry point in the house. The front foyer, the kitchen door, every window, the fireplace, the garage and the mudroom behind the laundry. Marvin called these sensors Phase One and neither he nor Ann believed that an ordinary security system would detect Tucker.

"We know that somehow he gains entry without tripping the typical house alarm," he had told her. "We might get lucky with Phase One, but I doubt it."

"That's a comforting thought," Ann said.

"Don't worry," Marvin said. "This guy's a master all right when it comes to security systems, but there are only two people in the world who can beat Phase Two and I'm one of them."

Ann just looked at him, not knowing whether to feel comforted or doomed.

"Phase Two will do the trick. You'll know."

"You didn't forget the grandfather clock in the foyer, did you?" she asked. She knew Tucker would save the clock for last. When the pendulum no longer moved, Ann would know that Tucker thought himself very close to his prey.

"Did that first thing," he said.

The system was Marvin's pride and joy. Phase Two was high tech surveillance equipment developed for the NSA by the German scientist Gunter Lutzen. The system could detect the cessation of any noise — when a heart stopped beating, when an electric cord was unplugged, when a cricket stopped chirping. Marvin had been one of a two-man installation team in a location known to them and the President and the head of NSA. His partner had retired and then disappeared. Marvin said too much counter-intelligence had messed up his head and he hadn't been heard from since.

Ann removed the pink ribbon from the shoebox and lifted the top envelope, noticing the military APO address. She removed the letter gently, carefully brushing away the dust.

Dear Jane, the letter began. The date was March 12, 1954. The Korean War had been over less than a year. The handwriting was barely legible.

God, how I miss you and the kids. It looks like I'll be back in the States before Thanksgiving if all stays calm in Korea. Keep your fingers crossed. The deal on the house sounds good. Go ahead and take our savings for the down payment. I can't imagine how great it will be to finally have our own place and if Bill and Mary do build next door, it'll be like old times again when all of this is finally over.

The remainder of the letter dealt with location, friends and longing. It was signed: *Don't forget who loves you. Neal'*

Ann folded the letter carefully and gently placed it on the bottom of the stack.

The second letter was dated March 14, 1954 and reflected the mood of a young family man looking forward to returning home from war. It was a portion of the third letter that caught Ann's attention. It was dated May 30, 1954.

'Dearest Jane,

Thanks for the cookies, although by the time they arrived, they were the best crumbs this unit ever fought over. All the guys want to meet you but that isn't ever going to happen. Glad the loan went through on the house. *Tell Bill that I expect him to take care of grilling the steaks every Saturday night and I'll do the chicken every Sunday. Did you flip to see whose house gets the pool? Just kidding. I know we can't afford that. Later, maybe! The fallout shelter is a must. If it's done during construction, it shouldn't cost an arm and a leg.'*

Ann stopped reading. She knew nothing about a fallout shelter. They were aware when they moved in that the house had been refurbished several times. The stiff linoleum, broken and chipped had been the first to go, followed quickly by the harvest gold refrigerator and dishwasher. She remembered every detail of the renovation, every broken fingernail and sore muscle but she had no recollection of a fallout shelter.

She continued reading: *'We keep hearing over here that the cold war is easing, but every time you turn around, there's news of some new atomic weapon. We saw pictures yesterday of the first nuclear powered sub and my buddy, Leon, who's from Pittsburgh said that an atomic power plant is going to be built there. Sounds to me like the big guys don't think it's over.'*

Ann wondered how her fear of being murdered by a deranged killer compared to the fear of death by nuclear bomb.

'Yes, I think a shelter under each house might just save us. The builder ought to be able to connect our houses by a narrow tunnel. Ask him. At least if we have to go underground, the kids can all play together and you and me can beat the pants off of Bill and Mary at rummy. If the shelter costs more than we can qualify for, I know Mom and Dad would help out.' He signed his letter: *'I love you, you beautiful woman. Neal'*

Ann returned the letter to the box, carefully tied the ribbon and began to think about the shelter. Where was it? Had it been connected to the house next door? The one on the right or the one on the left? Was it still accessible?

She had been in the room for only two hours when she noted action on the Phase Two monitor. Her heart raced as she glanced at Phase One. Nothing. All lights on Phase One were OK. There was no indication of entry. However, the lights on Phase Two were going off one by one. All the sounds within her house were being shut off. She watched as the last red light on the Phase Two monitor went out – it was the one on the pendulum. Silence in the house. Complete and total silence. He was here.

The feeling of safety when the shelter was complete was now quickly replaced by unease that steadily turned to terror. What if no one came to help? What if Tucker had somehow learned that she had outwitted him and decided to wait her out – however long it took? Perspiration beaded across her forehead, the hairs bristled on the back of her neck as the image of him thrusting a knife into her gut brought her to near panic. She could see the evil in his eyes as clearly as she had that day in the courtroom. Suffocating under the weight of her own horror, she thought of what he might do to her and wondered if she would die quickly or slowly before he finished.

Just as she felt she could no longer breathe, an inner resolve forced her to pick up Allen Smith's card. She grabbed the cell phone. She wasn't sure why she didn't push the red button to summon police. With fingers trembling, she dialed the number. The phone only rang once when a comforting voice answered: "Smith here."

"Mr. Smith, this is Ann Sayre."

"Yes, I know."

"How?"

"Caller I.D. is relatively simple technology, even for the FBI," he said.

"I'm glad you called. Are you in the fort?"

"How did you know about the fort?"

"Marvin Langley. Sorry! He confided in me as soon as he finished your project. He still works for us on a contract basis. We've been watching the house ..."

"How?"

"Ever notice the telephone truck across the street. All the comforts of home and enough technology and fire power to launch all-out war."

"I can't believe it. I thought it might be him," she said. "But I thought surveillance was cancelled."

"It was, but I had several weeks of leave I didn't know what else to do with ..."

Ann watched the monitors and saw nothing. Confused, she asked. "Why?"

"Guess I just couldn't let this happen. The guy's a monster and I personally think you've been right all along. For some reason, only he knows why, he left you until last and was playing with you and with us too — waiting for just the right minute.

"He's here, in the house now," she whispered as if the sound-proof walls would betray her.

His voice was calm. "He can't be. There's no way. We would have seen. I've got every access monitored."

Panic rose again in her throat as she told him about the letters and the fallout shelter. "Holy Shit! Of course" he screamed into the phone. "Don't move, don't call, and don't do anything. Just hang tight to that gun. Remember code words 'Bacon and Eggs'". No talk, no entry, no access, no nothing without that code. GOT IT!"

"Yes" she whispered. "I think he moved in next door."

"I know." The connection was broken.

Ann had barely enough time to dwell on Smith's words when she felt tremors through the floor and walls, much like the way an Air Force jet breaking the sound barrier occasionally assaulted her china cabinet. She looked at the TV monitors. Nothing. On the sound monitors, the needles were straining against the far right of the red zone. The silence of the night had been punctured. The tremors continued for what seemed an eternity and then they stopped. She prayed that somehow Allen Smith had come through and Randolph Tucker had been silenced, forever. She waited and prayed, the powerful gun clutched firmly in both hands, finger on the trigger, ready for one last defense.

The soft ring of the phone jolted her. She pushed the bottom, hoping to hear just one word.

Afraid to speak, she waited. The deep voice spoke. "Bacon and Eggs. It's OK to open the door.

"Oh my God," was all she said before she pulled back the massive lock on the door and admitted five members of the Special Unit, dressed in black boots, black uniforms and black masks with only slits to see and breathe through.

The tallest of them ripped off his mask to reveal the most beautiful and welcome blond head of hair and friendly smile she had ever seen.

Allen Smith reached down and helped her stand up. Her hands trembled and he thought she might faint. With one hand under her elbow, he steadied her.

"Is it over?" she asked.

"It's over," he said. "But if you hadn't read those letters, he would still be in this house trying to find you.

"But if you knew he was next door, why didn't you just go in and get him."

"We didn't know he was there until the middle of last night — we just had enough time to map out a plan. By the time you made your call this morning, we were calling for back up, but since we knew you would be safe, we wanted to snare him in your house."

"Jesus." she said.

"He was too damn slippery. We couldn't afford to let him get away again."

"Is it really over?" she asked as if freedom from the torment Tucker had caused her for so long was beyond belief."

"Yes, it's over. There isn't much left of him. I'm afraid we'll have to re-do the stair walls and carpeting for you.

"Jesus," she said again, "that close?"

"Yup. Don't think about it," he said as he took her hand and led her out of the fort. "Oh yeah, we'll have to fix that hole in the basement laundry.

"The fallout shelter?" she asked.

"Yeah. Strange isn't it. A room built over forty years ago to protect a family from a bomb that might be dropped by Russia is used forty years later by some psycho to kill someone." He shook his head in disbelief. "Go figure."

"Can I borrow a mask?" she asked as they walked to the top of the stairs.

"Good idea." he said. "Don't look — maybe if your stomach isn't too upset, you'll have breakfast with me. I want to find out if we can borrow your plans for that fort — that is, if you haven't already patented them."

She knew he was teasing her and it felt good. "Upset? My stomach. Upset? Give me that mask!" she demanded as she pulled the mask down to cover her eyes. "And make noise, please. No silence. I need noise, and lots of it."

She let herself be led, then carried down the steps. "Why bacon and eggs," she asked.

He laughed a warm friendly laugh. "Nothing really clandestine. I was hungry as hell and it was the first thing that came to mind."

In the car, on the way to the Conrad Hotel where Allen had booked a room for her until the house was returned to normal, Ann leaned her head back and sighed.

"Will I ever feel safe again?" Without waiting for a response, she continued, "I remember reading somewhere once that safety is an illusion." She turned and looked at Allen. "Is that true?"

"I think you're as safe now as anyone else. No one is ever truly safe but most people don't have to deal with a Randolph Tucker in their lives."

"I suppose you're right," she said, "I'd really like to erase it all from my mind, but I know that'll take a long time."

The windshield wipers, turned on slow, were having almost a hypnotic effect on Ann. She yawned, fighting the urge to nod off. "I'm so damn tired, but I still have so many questions."

"For instance?" he asked as he steered the car under the Hotel's canopy.

"How did he know about the fallout shelter? And why did he wait so long between the last one and me?"

Allen turned the key off and looked at Ann. In the dim light from the hotel portico, he read the exhaustion on her face. A bellhop stood besides the car, waiting.

"Right now, we don't know and maybe we never will." He opened the door and motioned for the bellhop. "The investigation is still open, at least until some of these loose ends are tied up. We'll search the house next door and see what we come up with."

"You'll let me know what you find, won't you?"

"Of course," he said as he stepped out of the car.

They followed the bellhop to the elevator. He took both of her hands in his. "Get some sleep, Ann, a lot of sleep. In fact, sleep until noon or later and then call me."

She thanked him again. The elevator rose to the fifth floor and she followed the bellhop to her room. After he left, she turned the dead bolt, engaged the chain and placed a chair under the doorknob. When she awoke the next day to the ringing of the phone, it was already two in the afternoon and the only thing she remembered after locking the door the night before was slipping into bed.

It was Allen. "I see you took my advice."

"I slept like a baby," she said, as she tried to rub the burning from her eyes.

"Well, you made the early morning news. You're a hero in town."

"I'm alive, that's the only thing I am."

"Be glad for your instant celebrity status."

Allen explained that once the news broke, Miss Claudia Parker, County Librarian, called the Sheriff and told them about a thin, quiet man who had a real interest in building plans. Seems he spent a great deal of time in the library.

"I knew he was out there, I just knew it."

"Coincidentally, he was curious about Crompton Estates, your neighborhood, and particularly which, if any, of the homes had fallout shelters."

"Didn't she recognize him if he was in the library so much? After all, his face was plastered all over the front pages during the trial."

"No, his hair was different and he had a small moustache. Remember, though, his mother was a make-up artist."

"That's right, I remember now, and his father had been a locksmith."

"Wait till you hear this," Allan said, "Right after that call came in, a reporter for the Herald phoned headquarters with information he thought might be useful. Seems that a couple of months ago, his editor wanted a piece done on whether the passing of nuclear secrets to the Chinese might result in another cold war. So he did a series of articles, one of which dealt with the dread of nuclear fallout back in the 'fifties and America's rush to build fallout shelters in their homes. Guess which subdivision was built during that time and which the builder advertised as having the safest, strongest, — well you get the picture."

"I'll be God damned!"

"Then the house next door came up for sale and our monster had his fun, only it didn't turn out to be so much fun."

"So now we at least know how he found out about the fallout shelter, right?"

"Right, we just don't know why he waited so long. We probably never will."

"And what tipped him off that the house next door and mine might have connecting shelters?" She sat on the edge of the bed holding her head in one hand and the phone in the other. "I'll never be able to thank you enough."

"It turned out well," he said. "I'm off on assignment to D.C. for a week or so. When I come back, perhaps we can get together for dinner."

"I'd like that, I really would."

They said good-bye and Ann slipped back between the sheets and listened as the silence once again enveloped her like a soft fog on a winter morning. The silence and the 357 Magnum under her pillow told her she was safe.

ON CHEAT MOUNTAIN

Martha Montgomery let the water thaw her toes and fingers, numb after spending the afternoon sloshing through deep, wet snow looking for King, her two-year old yellow Lab and constant companion ever since she rescued him from the city pound when he was just a ball of fur no bigger than a skein of golden yarn. This wasn't like him. He never strayed more than a few yards from her and it certainly wasn't like him to run off when they were on the mountain.

She inhaled the humid air deep into her lungs, feeling it warm her inside, and wished she could dismiss all thoughts about her work as Assistant U.S. Attorney, Deputy Chief of Violent Crime, in Washington, D.C.

After her shower, she could dress warmer, eat a cup of soup and start searching again. With King missing, it didn't seem as urgent that she finish reviewing the latest evidence in the McGrath baby murder case, a case that had consumed her life for months. Ever since the nine-pound, five-week old brutalized baby had been discovered in a trashcan two blocks from the White House, Martha was consumed with seeing justice served and bringing some solace to the grieving parents.

With so many unanswered questions, only one arrest and pressure from higher up to solve the case quickly, she was emotionally drained. Something kept eating at her gut; how could she possibly prosecute a case when she felt that the wrong man had been charged? The report of a similar case in Richmond only added to her confusion. Two infants brutally murdered during a short span of time had to be more than a coincidence.

So much for the chance to spend the entire weekend with no interruptions, walks in the snow with King, time to go over the case again searching for the weak link. Now, nothing mattered except King. Where the hell was he?

In her frustration, she threw the soap and yanked the shower curtain aside. She asked herself the same question she had often asked, "How the hell did I get from Southwest Florida to Washington, D.C.?"

● ● ●

Marvin watched through the tiny crack beside the overhead light fixture, thrilled with her anger and the sheen of her wet skin, her long black hair clinging to her back. He thought she was much prettier and thinner than her pictures in the newspapers and on TV. He lay motionless, his breathing slow and silent, just as he had been taught to do in the Special Forces.

Careless fool I am, he thought, when he realized he had let snow fall from his pant cuffs as he climbed on the boxes in the small bedroom. He knew every inch of the cabin by heart; could move silently on his stomach over every room. Sometimes, he liked to scratch the floor lightly to mimic the sound of mice. He liked fooling her.

The dog was a problem that Marvin hadn't anticipated. When he first followed the woman from her townhouse to the mountain, when she first came to see the cabin, there was no dog. Then the damned thing came with her when she brought the boxes and furniture. It was too late. He was already in. He knew that some day he'd have to take care of that little problem just like he had done in Nam.

• • •

"Damn, where could he be?" *Better hurry*, Martha thought and wondered if maybe her excitement and feeling of contentment about the cabin and the mountain had been premature. "Nonsense," she told herself. Her head throbbed.

It was her old friend Neal Douglas who first tipped her off about the cabin while they were sharing war stories during lunch at the *San Souci*, a popular eatery on Connecticut Avenue in D.C. Neal was a lobbyist for an agri-business group and a retired Chief of the U.S. Forest Service. He and his wife, Betty, and Martha had been good friends for years.

The *San Souci* was crowded and conversation was lively. Usually the swank restaurant was full of lobbyists wooing legislators, gawking constituents hoping to catch a glimpse of the country's most famous political columnist and reporters looking for a story. So far no one recognized Martha. "Thank God," she thought. "No court room reporters on my tail today."

"Neal," Martha sighed. "Honestly, I'll burn out before I'm fifty." She stared off into space, tuning out the clatter of dishes and the loud voices. "I need an escape, a place where King and I can go on the weekend, a place where no one can find me."

They were both quiet while the waiter quickly cleared the table and poured coffee. When they were alone again

Neal leaned across the small table and whispered, "If you are serious — you won't believe this — but probably for a song, you might get lucky and pick up one of a dozen cabins that the Forest Service has been ordered to dispose of. And *I* can probably help you pull it off."

Martha set her cup down slowly. "I'd give anything to have a little place to escape to," she said. "Tell me about it."

Neal described the cabins on Cheat Mountain. Quiet, isolated and deep in the West Virginia woods. They would be sold very soon to avoid the fallout should the press learn that another powerful leader, the Chairman of the Senate Committee on Agriculture and Forestry, couldn't keep his fly zipped.

Martha giggled as Neal described how the Chairman's wife was a wee bit pissed off to discover her very busy husband had been busy indeed — but not on legislation. Instead, he was cavorting with his latest love at one of the cabins the Forest Service maintained on Cheat Mountain.

Martha laughed. "I guess nothing should surprise me any more, but I still have a hard time believing these guys are so stupid. How'd you find out?"

"Jerry called one day laughing his ass off. All the grief that old bastard from the Senate gave us over the years. Believe me, Martha, it couldn't happen to a nicer guy." Jerry Hukill had been Neal's Assistant Chief and now was in the Department's Congressional Liaison.

"So he got caught," she said. "What happened?"

"Well," Neal continued, "It didn't take the P.I. that the little wife hired long to discover what the cabins were used for and, in a rather revengeful mood, she promised not to reveal the name of her husband's lover in exchange for a huge settlement and a promise that every Forest Service cabin in the country would be auctioned to the general public.

Martha sipped her coffee. "This is so funny. So who's the bimbo, another intern?"

"No bimbo this time ..." Neal said, "I doubt seriously if she could bring the U.S. Department of Agriculture to its knees so quickly over some little ol' no-name bimbo."

"Then who ...?" Martha asked.

"Are you ready for this?"

"Don't tease."

"None other than the wife of the Chief Justice."

Martha bolted straight in her chair. "Jesus, Neal! You mean *The* Chief Justice? *Our* Chief Justice ... of *these* United States?"

"Yup, none other than ..."

Martha laughed aloud and quickly glanced around the dining room. "I'm speechless," she said.

Neal smiled. "Fun and games in the Nation's Capitol, my dear. Nothing new. Only the players change."

"No kidding," Martha said. "Not a word in the press?"

"Not one word."

The two old friends had a last cup of coffee and said good-bye. During the short cab ride to her office, Martha closed her eyes and imagined long walks in the woods and quiet time away from Washington.

Martha shut her office door and worked the system. Two calls to the Forest Service, mention Neal's name and her own position and the procurement specialist was more than willing to share with her the procedure, the timing, and, of course, what he thought a reasonable bid might be. She received the bid package the next morning and within two months was the proud owner of a rustic, well-maintained cabin on Cheat Mountain in West Virginia less than 215 miles from her Georgetown townhouse. She couldn't have been happier.

Almost overnight, Martha's weekend routine changed dramatically. A quick stop at the townhouse after work on Friday afternoon to get King and she was on Route #66 heading West, just ahead of rush hour traffic.

Martha had spent almost half of her forty-four years in the D.C. legal system, the last five as Deputy Chief of Violent Crimes. It was on the mountain that she finally found release from the shackles of her position, even if only for forty-eight hours at a time. It was why she was here again this January weekend even though heavy snow had been forecast. It was here that she felt totally safe until today when King wandered off.

• • •

Marvin didn't exactly remember all that happened in Richmond, only that the baby in the carriage in the park was screaming — kept screaming just like the first one. Why hadn't the mother who was not far away done something? He tried to shush the baby but it kept on crying. He ran down the alley cradling the tiny bundle, trying to get it to stop. The alley was deserted. Why wouldn't it stop crying?

• • •

"I wouldn't bother the ol' man in the cabin down from yours," the owner of the full-service gas station on the highway at the base of the mountain told Martha a week after she settled in. "Moved in right after you did, only he ain't so friendly."

"Maybe he just likes to be alone," Martha said. A recluse for a neighbor suited her just fine.

"Besides, after I'm here awhile," she added, "the locals will probably say the same about me."

"Nobody knows nothin' about him except that Bart over at the hardware said he's a little strange. Nosy old coot, I'd say ... came in here one day asking about who bought your cabin ..." but Martha had already turned and was walking into the station. He shrugged his shoulders and checked the dipstick again before slamming the hood down with a loud crash. He followed her into the station.

"Strange thing," he said, scratching his head with an oil-stained hand. "For as long as I can remember, this ol' mountain ain't seen much besides a steady procession of fancy cars with weekend visitors and then all of a sudden, we get two new permanent residents within a month of each other." Martha didn't let on that she knew to whom at least one of the fancy cars belonged.

"Thanks for your help," she said. "I doubt much traffic will be coming up to my cabin."

And now it was January and, just as predicted, the weather had turned vicious. The forecast called for another six to ten inches of snow on top of the six that fell the night before, with temperatures dropping down into the teens before morning. With the wind coming out of the

North, the chill factor might easily dip to below zero. Martha shivered at the thought of it.

The shower helped not only to warm her cold body, it helped her deal with the sense of dread that perhaps someone had coaxed the lovable dog away or that maybe he had wandered into an animal trap, was caught and in dreadful pain, maybe even dead. King never left her side for long; when he needed to go out he hurried, bounding clumsily down the front steps, took care of urgent business, sniffed a few moments, turned and scrambled up the porch stairs and into the front door to quickly take up his favorite place beside her feet. Not even a spooked rabbit could entice him from the area in front of the cabin and Martha always left the front door slightly ajar so he could nudge it open with his nose when he was ready to come back in.

Hurry! Hurry! She had to get back outside. She shivered again. Just as she was beginning to feel like she had eluded frostbite, she heard a sound from outside the bathroom door, closed to trap in the warm, moisture laden air. She quickly turned off the water and reached for a towel. She stood motionless, listening.

"King!" she called. "KING! Come boy!" Her voice loud now. "Is that you? COME!"

She expected to hear the familiar sounds of the frisky, ninety-five pound dog gallop down the hall and into the bathroom. She called again. There were no familiar dog sounds, only the slow drip, drip, drip of water falling from the overhead nozzle.

This time the unfamiliar sound came again, now louder and closer. She called out and again there was no response. Alarmed, Martha quickly judged the distance to the door. The hair bristled on her arms and goose bumps erupted on her arms and legs. She stood shivering; feeling a wave of dizziness come over her.

"Hello," she called out. "Is anyone there?"

Martha moved silently to the small table under the bathroom window and reached for her cell phone. Thank God, she thought as she pushed the power button. The flashing message screamed at her, LOW BATTERY!

"Jesus, I was going to charge it this morning."

She lunged at the door and flipped the lock, her legs feeling clumsy and awkward.

• • •

Marvin was angry with himself for letting his foot scrape on the floor. Stupid! Stupid! Stupid! He knew the military would have dismissed him for such an error. His whole platoon could have been blown to bits if the VC heard one little sound. Maybe his Sergeant wouldn't be so angry with him now if he knew how he had followed the DA, asked around until he found out how to buy the little cabin right down the mountain from hers. They'd have to give him a commendation if they could see how silently he could get in and out of the attic and the surveillance holes he had carved in the attic floor over every room.

It was just a matter of time before the woman suspected that the noises in the attic weren't mice. He was glad he thought to come down and turn the door handle – that would throw her off. Last weekend when he made the scratching noises, the dog had gotten up and walked to the hall door, its ears up, alert and listening. Marvin decided then to act the following weekend.

Dog should be frozen by now, he thought. Maybe he should have just killed it outright. But dogs didn't cry like babies.

• • •

With trembling fingers, Martha dressed as fast as she could, the wool socks and long underwear resisting her damp skin. There was only the sound of her rapid breathing. Jagged needles of sensation assaulted her skin as she sat on the toilet and pulled on her boots and watched as the knob on the door turned slowly.

"Who's there?" she commanded into the silence.

Bluffing, she yelled louder, "I have a gun!"

The Sig Sauer P-228 pistol lay unloaded in the bedroom only a few feet away, secure in an old wooden box on the top of the chest of drawers. Next to it, a box of bullets. She had never before felt the need for a loaded gun in the mountains. In fact, she had regarded her boss as being, up until this moment, way beyond paranoid when he insisted she carry it.

The doorknob was now still and Martha crouched in the corner assessing the three options she had, all equally lousy. Stay holed up in the bathroom until whoever or whatever had invaded her cabin was gone, and God only knows how long that might take; try to squeeze out of the bathroom window; or exhibit exemplary bravery and barge through the doorway and meet the unknown head on. Option number one seemed the wisest, at least until she could think more clearly.

An hour passed while she sat listening, hearing only night sounds from the woods mingled with the sound of blood pulsing in her ears. She rejected the second option once she compared the width of the window with the girth of her hips. "Damn," she whispered, cussing a year of fast food lunches and heavy take-out dinners. The image wasn't humorous, although she was sure there were others who would find great delight in seeing a photo spread across the front page of the *Washington Post* of the often-controversial Assistant U.S. Attorney, dead *or* alive with her rear end jammed tightly in the bathroom window.

Martha quietly opened the medicine cabinet. Sleeping tablets, deodorant, bug repellent. Hardly an arsenal of survival equipment. Her eyes fell upon the small package of razor blades.

She flipped the lock on the bathroom door and opened the door slowly, sharp blade poised ready to strike. In the dim light of the hall she could barely see. The little lamp with the black bear cub as its base, a gift from her dad, sat solidly on the hall table, casting a familiar warm glow on the floor.

The front door was closed even though she was sure she had left it open for King. She pushed the bathroom door open wide, moved quickly into the bedroom and locked the door. For a brief moment, she wondered if she were alone.

Her fright thrilled him. He watched as she moved quickly to the dresser and the gun.

One dresser drawer was opened halfway, its contents in disarray. She stared at it. Had she opened it earlier? Fear began to strip her of her usual composure. Raw chills crept along her back. Someone had been, or maybe still was, in the cabin. Martha quickly loaded the gun, not letting her eyes stray from the closet and the bed. She opened the door slowly and moved cautiously through the rooms, checking and rechecking every closet and cabinet, looking under the bed twice. When she was satisfied that she was alone, she used the hall phone and called the local Sheriff's office.

Sheriff Harvey Laughton sounded like he had been awakened from a deep sleep. "We don't have much problem up here, Miss Montgomery," he said. "Could've been the wind."

Martha wasn't one given to spells of hallucination. Nor was she accustomed to being dismissed as if she were a schoolgirl with an overactive imagination. She was tired and bristled at his casual manner. "The wind, even up here, Sheriff," she said sarcastically, "doesn't turn door handles, does it?"

Best way to calm an overwrought female, the Sheriff concluded, and to get back to his nap was to send an officer to check things out and to file a report on her missing dog. "Keep your doors locked, ma'am, and I'll have a man up there before you know it."

Martha thanked him curtly and slammed down the phone. *What does he think I am, some dumb woman out of control?* It took the deputy twenty minutes to get there and Martha used the time to search every inch of the cabin once again. She noted that even the sounds of the always-active mice in the attic were absent. *Must have scared even them*, she thought.

Deputy Creighton was over-weight, his face round and plump with a thin mustache resting solidly on his upper lip. Martha thought he might be twenty-two, if that, and wondered about an investigation in the hands of a kid. Although he was mannerly, Martha's fears about his youth were not allayed. His slight accent with a twang led her to believe he was raised not far from Cheat Mountain. In spite of her skepticism, he appeared to take his job seriously and seemed anxious to take her report.

"Tell me exactly what happened," he asked, his fresh yellow pad and pencil poised for note taking. She told him everything, how King never strayed far from the cabin, that he hadn't come back in after he had gone out around two o'clock this afternoon, the noise she heard while she was in the bathroom, the doorknob turning and the mice in the attic. When he was finished writing, he walked through the cabin, checking every closet, under the bed, behind furniture, just as Martha had done.

"Are you going to check for prints?" she asked.

"Doesn't seem to be much reason for that ..." he said.

"But the bathroom door ..."

"There's five inches of fresh snow out there Miss Montgomery, but there's only one set of tracks pointing away from the cabin and one set pointing toward it and you can hardly see 'em now, snow's comin' down so fast."

He paused to check his notes. "'And ...'" he said, as if adding conviction to his conclusion, "look in the front hall and all through the cabin, there's no melted snow on the floor."

Martha could see quickly where this was going.

"Doesn't it stand to reason ..." he said, "... if someone had come in, in this weather, they would've had to carry in some snow on their shoes?"

Martha looked down at his feet. He had removed his boots and left them at the front door and he had shaken the snow off his coat before he came in. *He was right. But how ... ?*

"What about the attic?" He asked. "Any access?"

They both glanced at the ceiling. "Just a trap door through the second bedroom which serves as a store room. I would think it is nailed shut. I've never been up there. Nothing there except mice, *very* noisy mice."

"Only kind there is," he said. "All the same, I think I'll have a look."

"Fine," she said and went to the small kitchen to put water on for tea while Creighton crossed the hall and opened the door to the storage room. A few moments later, he walked into the kitchen.

"Nothin' suspicious there," he told her confidently, a small smile of satisfaction on his face. He wouldn't have even checked the room if he weren't so sure it would make the nervous woman with the vivid imagination feel better. "Make her think you've checked every inch of that place," the Sheriff had suggested, "Make her feel good enough so's she can sleep all night and not bother us again."

Creighton's inspection of the storage room had therefore become a mere formality. Had he walked amongst the boxes, he would have seen the small puddle of water on the floor directly under the trap door.

Martha handed him a cup of tea. "Milk? Lemon? Sugar?"

The delicate teacup was almost lost in his pudgy hand. He held the writing tablet in the other. "No thanks, this is fine," he said. "Kind of you. Thanks."

"Let's go over this again; you went out to look for your dog and then came back, right?" And so she told him again, told him that she had walked close to two miles before she got so cold she couldn't go on. "I had to stop then because I was afraid I wouldn't make it back."

Martha couldn't tell if the Deputy was really intent on investigating the disappearance of the dog and the mysterious activity she reported or whether he was play-acting. He stood with one foot on the chair, resting the teacup on his knee. Had he watched too many detective shows on TV and rehearsed the appropriate stance?

He set the teacup down, made another notation on the tablet, and said, "The tracks I see are yours and some very faint animal tracks — could be your dog — going off into the woods to the South."

Martha took another tea bag from the tin canister. The phone rang.

"For you," she said as she handed him the portable phone.

"Yes, sir! Right, sir! No, sir!"

"JESUS!" Martha said under her breath. "Can't he say anything else?"

• • •

Frustrated and impatient, with exhaustion creeping into her bones, Martha sat down at the table and sipped the warm tea. She listened as the young Deputy spoke to his superior, her thoughts on King. How lonely she had been before she found him. The ever-increasing pressures of her position had taken their toll until King came into her life and she bought the cabin. It was as if they had been sent to help her get her emotional and physical act together.

Creighton moved toward her and patted her shoulder. A wide grin spread on his face. "Wow, that's really good news, sir."

Martha's heartbeat quickened. What was it … ?

"Yes, sir, I'll tell her straight away. Yes, sir, I'm sure she'll be very happy to hear the news."

Martha jumped from the kitchen chair and took the phone.

The tone of the Sheriff's voice was more compassionate than when she first spoke with him. "Folks over near Glady, 'bout eleven miles from here, just called the station to report they found a dog — description matches yours, cold and tired, but otherwise apparently OK.

"Thank God." Martha yelled into the phone. "Eleven miles? Jesus, how the hell … ?"

Martha heard another phone ring and the Sheriff begged off. "Gotta get that other line. Creighton can fill you in on the details." He hung up.

The deputy was now writing fast and speaking. "If he's yours … now there's no guarantee, but sounds pretty much like yours, someone could've picked him up on the road and he jumped out when they stopped somewhere. No telling."

"You're sure he's OK?" Martha asked, relief flooding her face and tears rising.

"Folks said they found him huddled, half frozen up against their garage and they took him in. He's thawing out now in front of their fireplace and seems to be in pretty good shape considering."

"Thank God."

"Only thing is ... ," he said. "You'll have to wait 'til tomorrow to see him. Sheriff said we'd be glad to send a car for him and bring him home. Maybe he'll let me bring him back up to you."

Martha smiled, feeling somewhat guilty that she had wondered about the skill of the law enforcement staff on Cheat Mountain.

"That would be nice, thank you. I'd like that."

They stood on the front porch shaking hands, the snow now falling fast, heavy, wet, and turning the mountain landscape into an artist's dream, frothy white upon white. Occasionally, the moon broke through the clouds and sent slivers of light gleaming through the trees turning each snowflake into a sparkling crystal

"Sure you don't want to come into the station and spend the night, Miss Montgomery?"

She wiped snow from her face. "Thanks, but I'll be just fine."

"I think you will", he said confidently as he headed through the deep snow toward the patrol car. "Nothin' much happens up here in these mountains."

"That's comforting," she yelled over the wind as he opened the car door. "You drive safely!" She watched the taillights dim as the car moved cautiously down the driveway and turned onto the curving mountain road. Until the plows came through the next day, she knew that no car could make it up to the cabin. She would just have to wait to see King.

• • •

He watched from behind a tree as the car disappeared down the mountain road and the woman went inside the cabin and closed the door. In the quiet of the night, he heard the dead bolt. He had made another mistake in judgment. He should have known she'd call the Sheriff. Now he'd have to decide what to do. He inched his way along the narrow path. It wound back and forth like a maze and eventually led to within 100 feet of the woman's cabin. He was glad the woman didn't have a baby. The snow made him think of his mother. They used to laugh and make angels in the snow before she let that lazy bum get her knocked-up every nine months.

Marvin couldn't remember a time, after his father was killed and his mother brought her new husband home, when she wasn't pregnant. He still woke up at night hearing her whine, "Marvin, pick up the baby! Marvin, the baby's crying! Marvin, the baby needs changing!" He couldn't remember a time when the house didn't smell like baby piss, baby vomit or the choking stench of ammonia from the uncovered pail of soiled diapers. He thought about making a baby with the woman and wondered if it would cry all the time. Would she make him change it? Feed it? Watch it all the time?

• • •

Martha checked every door and window again. Once satisfied, she dropped, totally fatigued, into the recliner by the front window, loaded gun and phone resting on her lap. Had she imagined the entire episode in the bathroom? *After all, when you are cold and tired and hungry, the imagination can play some pretty wild and terrifying tricks.* Isn't that what she often said on cross-examination?

And the worry about King ... Tomorrow I'll call the office and finish the letter to Mom that I started last night.

She turned off the lamp and watched the snowflakes blow onto the window, then melt, forming little rivers that ran down the pane and puddled on the windowsill. She listened carefully. Soon there was only the sound of the wind and the furnace, going steadily now, and the renewed activities of the mice in the attic. She closed her eyes and began to doze. It was thirty minutes past eleven. She smiled as she remembered King when he was a puppy; how he loved to slip into the bathroom when she was bathing, dragging and shaking her discarded clothing and wet towels as he scampered through the house. She would be so happy to have him back. She was tired and sleep came quickly.

PLAYGROUND OPEN FOR SUMMER

Brandon Mitchell swiveled the comfortable leather recliner away from the TV screen, faced the window and watched the two workers who reminded him of Mutt and Jeff construct the *Play Safe Home Playground*, cost $2000 parts & labor and built to last, the ad had proclaimed: "For your kids, their kids, and even *their* kids." Only after he had personally scrutinized every playground product on the market with the tenacity of a food inspector, did Brandon decide that *Play Safe* indeed was safe enough for his grandchildren Kimberly and Austin.

He smiled as he imagined the seven and six year-olds hanging from the bars or scooting through the vertical maze to the sliding board, giggling and waving to him to be sure he watched them. In the ranking of cherished family events, the children's annual summer visit rivaled his and Maura's visit north each Christmas. Oh, how they hated to see the children leave – plans for the next year's visit were begun almost as soon as the tears dried.

But this year he alone would meet them at the plane and he alone would fix their favorite Mickey Mouse ear waffles each morning and he alone would tuck them in at night. Maura's breast cancer had struck suddenly. Could it really have been three years since she died? Gone so quickly. She loved Kimberly and Austin with a passion equal to his own.

He watched through the window as the workers hefted the two-by-fours into place. He knew Maura would approve the expenditure of two thousand dollars on play equipment, even if he did have to pay for it in installments. He was sure of it.

Another son, John, unmarried, lost himself sometime back, severing family ties — a heartless act that almost killed Maura before the cancer took her. *Was it their fault? How could a loving son just leave, no note, no good-byes, no "I hate you!"* No nothing. The cancer consumed Maura with an evil vengeance, but the loss of a son ripped into her heart. When the Christmas card she mailed to him, the one with the tender inscription: *To A Special Son*, with ten lines of '*I remember when ....*' was returned with *No Forwarding Address* stamped in bold letters on the envelope, the killer inside her, as if sensing a greater vulnerability, delivered its fatal blow. She died three days later cradled in Brandon's arms, a photograph of her lost son clutched in her hands.

From that day on, Brandon devoted his attention to Austin and Kimberly and soon became the model grandparent who drove friends crazy, pulling out wallet and photo albums at the very mention of children or family. He had become one of those obnoxious, bragging, loving grandparents and he was proud of it.

A part-time job at the local hardware store kept Brandon's mind occupied and even permitted a small savings account. In his spare time he tended his garden, kept the house in good repair and bowled or fished with his old bachelor buddy Zeke.

Together, they joined the seniors' league down at the "Ten Pin Alley" and on Wednesday night took on the competition. Sunday afternoons, if weather cooperated, they filled the cooler with soft drinks and a few beers, loaded the rods and some bait into Zeke's small boat and rowed out into the middle of Sunrise Lake to test their luck, which usually wasn't too good. "Doing lots of fishing, not too much catching," Zeke would holler to anyone who came close.

Zeke had grown up on the streets of Brooklyn, a career fireman with bad lungs and skin scarred by flames. Brandon thought him a good man and a good friend and while Brandon pruned his roses and planted the trays of KMart's season-special seedlings he bought every chance he got, Zeke polished the '58 Corvette he affectionately called "Babe".

"There isn't gonna be any paint left on that car if you keep polishing it," Brandon teased. But Zeke kept right on waxing and rubbing until the chrome trim gleamed like sterling and not a speck of dust or a streak of wax was visible. They enjoyed their time together; Zeke told stories of tragic fires and heroic rescues and Brandon shared news about his grandkids' first teeth, school grades, and vaccinations.

"Enjoy 'em when they're little," Zeke advised, "Cause as soon as they get in high school, grandparents aren't high on their priority." Brandon couldn't imagine that; couldn't imagine not having Kimberly and Austin running towards him and jumping into his lap, laughing as they pulled his ears, hugged his neck, teased him about his wrinkles and nose hairs, planning their outings. He just couldn't imagine that at all! He closed his eyes and began to doze.

A knock on the window jolted Brandon awake. A glance at the wall clock told him he had slept through lunch and into the afternoon.

The short worker motioned him outside. They walked across the lawn toward the new structure which rose proud and majestic out of the ground. Six-by-six uprights, two-by-four cross beams, and metal bolts that gleamed bright in the Florida sun. Brandon thought it magnificent and wished the children were arriving today just so he could hear their whoops of surprise. How in the world could he keep the secret? Well, he thought to himself, I'll just have to manage, that's all there is to it.

"Thought you might want to check it before we attached the swings."

Brandon ran his hands over the smooth wood and examined one of the joints, stretching his neck to look at the connections overhead.

"Looks good. I want to make absolutely sure every bolt is tightened down."

The worker smiled. "Got little kids, huh?"

"At my age, not hardly, but I've got two grandkids coming for a visit later this month and I want this to be perfect." He started to reach for his wallet and their pictures and decided against it.

"This thing'll stand up to a Category 5 hurricane," the worker said, "I wish they built houses this solid. I'd buy one tomorrow."

"Safety first," Brandon said as he explained Kimberly's gymnastic schedule and Austin's soccer practices.

The workers were impatient to leave but too polite to interrupt.

"Instead of rushing back and forth on bikes and roller skates like we used to do and like our kids used to do," Brandon said, "kids now are hustled from one extra-curricular activity to another, meeting schedules that used to be reserved for adults, schedules that spawn ulcers."

"You got that right, sir," the tall worker replied. "Whatever happened to good old summer vacations when *lazy* was what it was all about, when the most exciting thing we did on a hot, muggy day was bum a quarter and go get an ice cream or sit in a frigid theatre watching a Grade B movie."

The short worker nodded his head. "Yeah, and if we got rained out, we'd gather around somebody's dining room table for a fierce game of Monopoly."

"But then," Brandon said, "This is a different generation than when I was a kid back in Philly."

"You got that right," the tall worker said. "They got drugs and stuff like gangs to worry about now."

Brandon nodded in agreement, then stood back and surveyed the equipment.

"If it meets with your OK, Mr. Mitchell, we'll be going along," said the tall worker as he produced a clipboard and pen for Brandon to sign. "Right here."

Brandon shook hands with both of the workers. "It's fine. It's really fine. I mean it, I really appreciate the good job you did."

As they headed toward their truck, the tall one turned and yelled, "Enjoy them kids."

"Thanks again, you bet I will," he whispered to himself.

He sat in the swing, hoping that maybe it creaked just a little, like the old swings in the park near his grandparent's home back in Philadelphia, but there was only the sound of his breath and the soft sound of the summer breeze easing through the maples. Next week he'd go buy some huge ribbon to make bows and large paper on which he could print SURPRISE! before he picked them up at the airport. Matt hadn't made their reservations yet, but it was summer and they weren't traveling on a holiday weekend so space shouldn't be a problem. Matt had always had a bit of procrastinator in him, but he usually made up for it some other way, although at times the cost of the tickets increased because he put things off too long. *Always busy, climbing the company ladder,* Brandon thought. Work hard to pay the bills, buying expensive clothes for Kimberly and Austin, pay what Brandon thought was much too much for private lessons. But that wasn't any of his business so he never said anything. *That's life in the fast lane, as they say now,* thought Brandon. He was very proud of Matt.

He stopped the swing when he saw "Babe" purr around the corner and come to an abrupt stop in the driveway. Zeke got out and closed the door gently.

"Hey, granddad, I like your new toy. Can I come play?"

Brandon laughed, "Sure, Zeke, but first park that thing in the shade before the reflection blinds me."

"It's a fine structure," Zeke said as he walked around and under the playground, inspecting it closely. "Those kids are darned lucky."

Brandon slipped out of the swing and turned toward the house. Zeke followed close behind.

"Let's get some good ice tea like Maura used to make us. Or a nice cold beer."

"Sounds like a plan, my friend," Zeke said.

They sat at the kitchen table telling old stories and drank iced tea and ate cookies until dusk. Zeke never liked to have "Babe" out after dark and when he noticed the time, he left in a hurry.

"Thanks for the tea, pal. See ya' Wednesday evening. You drive?" He always asked even though it had long ago been agreed that Brandon drove on Wednesday evenings — "Babe" was too valuable to be parked at the Ten Pin, day or night.

Brandon was getting ready for bed when he first noticed the blinking light on his answering machine. He pushed the *PLAY* button. The deep voice spoke quickly, "Hi Dad, it's me, Matt. Call me as soon as you can, we've got a little problem with schedules. Talk to you later. Bye."

● ● ●

Brandon wondered if he had been right. Had Matt waited so long that seats were unavailable on any flight? He sat down and called his son's number. The answering machine clicked on which usually meant Matt was in a meeting or doing something and couldn't be disturbed. At the beep, Brandon spoke slowly, never comfortable talking to a machine, "Matt, it's Dad. I'll be up late, call me back when you can."

He put the phone gently in its cradle, walked through the house turning off the lights and then slowly climbed the steps to the bedroom. He pushed away all thoughts that Kimberley and Austin might not visit. He removed the old crocheted bedspread and folded it neatly just as Maura taught him to do, placing it carefully on the Lane treasure chest, a gift from her mother and father when she graduated from college.

The soft mattress felt good under his back. It had been a long day. He wondered what problem the kids had with schedules. Maybe they would arrive earlier than planned. If so, he was sure glad he had the play equipment installed today. He stared at the picture he kept on the dresser; Austin balancing on one foot on the top rail of the Jenkins' monkey bars and Kimberly hanging upside down by her knees, her braces sparkling in the warm Florida sun. How much had they grown since Christmas?

He let his thoughts wander and he remembered last summer. There was a similar problem with schedules then, too, and Matt even hinted something to the effect that the kids just weren't that excited about coming at all. Brandon knew that couldn't be. How could it? Maybe someone else's grandkids, but not his! They always had so much fun on their visits. He remembered how hurt he had been. Just the thought that they might not be able to visit had left him in despair but fortunately the schedules worked out OK and when they arrived, it was nothing but two weeks of fun and games right up until he put them on the airplane for the trip back North.

Brandon whispered in the quiet of the lonely bedroom as if Maura were lying beside him, holding his hand, just as she always did before she fell asleep. "Remember the time we hired that guide and went fishing deep in the Everglades and Austin fought that little snook until his stomach hurt and he couldn't wait to get back to the motel and call home." Brandon turned toward the empty space beside him. "And how about the time when we drove with them to New York and how you got upset with me when I took them up in that helicopter so they could see all of Manhattan."

He made a mental note to get up early and maybe catch Matt before he left for the office. He just couldn't believe that they wouldn't want to come visit. What about the planned trip to London and Paris when they each graduated from High School? He was their granddad, after all, and a promise was a promise. Placing two fingers to his lips and then gently onto the face of Maura in their wedding picture on the nightstand, he let negative thoughts fade as he fell into a restless sleep.

He awoke before dawn, fixed breakfast and spent the day close to the phone.

It was late in the evening when Matt called. "Dad, we really have a problem with the kids' visit." Brandon was silent as Matt spoke rapidly about how it turned out that the kids only had three days in between *this* practice and *that* camp and how they didn't want to disappoint him and how he didn't think it worth while to spend close to $800 to fly them down for just three days ... but he would, except ..."

Brandon sat down in the recliner and tried to focus, feeling the tightening in his throat. Matt's words became a blur.

"Hey, I understand." Brandon said.

"You'll be up at Christmas, before then if we can work it out, and you'll see them then," Matt said, "I'll be glad to fly you up here now if you want."

"No problem, son, I'll take a rain-check."

"Great! Kimberly was really worried that you'd be upset."

"I'm disappointed, of course, but hey, don't worry about it." He was suffocating and just wanted the call to be over. "Tell them how much I love them and will be looking forward to my Christmas visit."

"OK, Dad, gotta run. Really sorry."

"Take care son, see you soon."

Brandon Mitchell remembered he had forgotten to make the bed when he got up that morning. He climbed the stairs slowly and walked into the room in which his two children were conceived and in which their mother had died. He lifted the spread carefully and, just as Maura taught him, placed it exactly square on the bed, making sure that each pillow was carefully covered and the hem was just one inch from the floor all the way around. He stopped and looked around the room. He could feel Maura's approval. His eyes filled with tears as he turned off the light and went downstairs.

• • •

In the garage, he had to move boxes and garden tools to reach the powerful chainsaw. He opened the cap and filled the reservoir with gas. The fumes smelled good and familiar. He walked into the warm night air across the lawn toward the *Play Safe Home Playground.*

The cord offered no resistance to the distraught man and the sound of the powerful tool smashed through the neighborhood with the force of a tornado. Brandon could visualize the overhead bars and swings crashing to the ground one by one.

Sue and Tom Jenkins from across the street at first thought they were hearing a neighbor's television but when they realized the commotion came from the Mitchell's yard, they raced out of their house and ran toward the noise. Brandon was standing beside the large play equipment, holding the roaring chainsaw in his right hand and wiping tears from his eyes with his left.

Tom Jenkins approached cautiously and yelled, "Sure you want to do that, Mitch?" He reached one hand slowly toward his friend and neighbor.

Brandon lowered the chainsaw to his side, and then turned the switch to silence it. "No, I don't," he said as he stared at the ground. "Thought for a minute if I ripped it apart, the pain of losing Maura and the kids not coming down might vanish."

Tom took the chain saw from Brandon and Sue put her arms around him. "We know how you miss her, Mitch," she said, "we miss her too."

"Stupid! Stupid! Stupid!" Brandon scolded as he turned to walk toward the house. "How could I have been so stupid?" Sue and Tom followed him into the kitchen.

"How 'bout a cup of tea with an old man who's losing it," Brandon asked as he slumped at the table, head in his hands, looking weary and very tired.

The three friends sat around the table for close to an hour, drinking tea and talking. Only when Sue and Tom felt confident that Brandon would be OK did they stand to say goodnight.

"Sure you're gonna be OK, Brandon?" Sue asked as she hugged him and kissed his cheek.

"Yeah, I'm sure," he replied and smiled. "Thanks. Just a momentary loss of sanity."

The phone in the hall interrupted their departure. "Get that, would you, Tom?" Brandon asked, "I'm not sure I can take any more bad news today."

Tom returned to the kitchen a few minutes later and winked at his wife. "Mitch," he said, a broad smile erupting on his face, "I think you'd better take this call. We'll check in with you in the morning."

"Who was that?" Sue asked as they crossed the lawn and passed through the long shadows cast by the full moon shining on the massive playground.

"That was Matt. Seems as if there was a mistake or something in the dates for the kids' activities and they'll be here day after tomorrow. Mitch is going to be one happy camper tonight. That playground is going to get a lot of use, come two days from now."

Brandon took half of the steps two at a time, and then finished the climb more slowly. *Slow down, old man*, he thought, feeling his heart pound much too fast. He lay down on the bed, happy and exhausted, eyes still burning, grateful that he had not committed an act that he would have regretted for the rest of his life.

He took the picture of Maura from the nightstand and held it to his chest. "They're coming, Maura, they're really coming." As he drifted off to sleep he muttered, "I miss you so much."

HOME SWEET HOME

Gracious me! I thought Reverend Manning was never going to get this service going. That man is slow as molasses on an iceberg. Always was. Always will be. But we all love him just the same. Cut the chatter Manning and try to keep the *"I remember her when..."* stories to a few and get this over quickly. They have to have me back at the Ranch by sundown. That's a definite! No maybe about it! Sundown!

Goodness, this place is packed. What a beautiful day for a service. Just what I wished for. Ribbons of early sunlight glowing through the stained glass window that I have loved for these many years. How many years has it been? Fifteen? Twenty? A lifetime! And the people here today. I haven't seen this many people in church since the Thompson's twins were killed.

I can't believe my eyes. Is that old Doc Summerville over there in the second pew? What in the world is he doing here? I wouldn't exactly call him a hypocrite but he's been angry ever since we refused to pay that ridiculous bill he sent us after Cathy's appendectomy. That's got to be sixty years ago at least. Poor child, she almost died by the time they got that old geezer on the phone and then he had the nerve to charge extra because it was a Sunday. Now my sweet Cathy has grown children of her own. Time does fly, doesn't it? Or perhaps I should say *did* fly.

Long services always did bother me and I know those little grandchildren's bottoms will be wiggling like the tails of a litter of hungry puppies. Doesn't matter whether it's a wedding or a funeral. I always thought "sweet and simple" was the ticket — get it over with so the couple or the dear departed could get on with their lives — well, *lives* in the case of the couple, and on with whatever the Lord has in store for the departed. My goodness, who could ever forget Granddad Sayre's service? Must have gone on for at least two hours; thought I was going to pass out. Late August and before the improvement fund was fat enough for an air conditioner. I'm beginning to feel a little like that today. Just a little stuffed and cramped.

Oh, I hope they hurry. Get on with it. I'd like to be in the Lake by sundown, always my favorite time of the day what with the ducks feeding and the deer appearing out of nowhere to gather at the edge of the water. Oh my goodness, it was most romantic when Ralph and I stood beside the lake that day over sixty years ago. He was so nervous he dropped the ring and got his best trousers all muddy and I tried not to laugh and he told me later he was afraid I would say no. Silly man! He was the best catch in all of Pendleton County and when we wed and moved to the Ranch, I was the envy of every single woman for miles around. After everyone left and we cleaned up the last crumbs of the three-tier wedding cake that Aunt Emma made, that dear sweet husband grabbed my hand and led me, almost running, down to the lake, held me close to his chest and whispered that he now knew what *home-sweet-home* meant.

Every one of those anniversaries, except when he was away to war and when he got so sick he couldn't leave the house, he'd take my hand and lead me down the path, under the grape arbor, with those bushes just hanging heavy with muscadines, down past the crape myrtle bushes full of bloom and kiss me just like he did that day he proposed. And he'd always say. "Helen, *you* make this *home-sweet-home*."

Oh look, here come the boys down the aisle. Funny, I still think of them as my little boys even though they're both way past middle age. Strange how a few years back all of a sudden I couldn't remember their ages. Once was a time when I could rattle all three of them out real fast, Randy, born 1938, the quiet, timid one who grew up to become the bossy, loud one. Wonder if he knows how miserable he's made my life the last two years with his do this, Mom, and you can't do that, Mom, like I was one of his underlings. Guess the Marines and Reba did that to him. I wouldn't be surprised if he rewrote the service today to suit himself. Funny thing about mothers, they love their children no matter what, but he sure could make me mad. Look! There's Reba. No tears in her eyes and probably counting their share right now. Oh gracious, that's not so nice of me, is it? I should be more charitable, shouldn't I, especially on my last day in church.

Now let's see, where was I? Oh yes, the boys. I was thinking about the boys. Next came Mikie in 1939 less than a year after Randy. Poor little Mikie, so tiny, fighting that nasty croup all winter long. Got so weak he couldn't nurse and we thought we'd lose him. But he's a fighter. I mean that in a good way. Always fighting for what is good and helping other people. Don't know what I'd have done without Mikie. Trouble is he never could stand up to Randy. Even when Randy and Reba showed up at the Ranch a couple of years ago and without even asking started pulling some of the old furniture out of the storeroom in the barn and hauling it up to their new place in Delaware, Mikie was so angry but he never said anything to Randy. "Mom," he said to me after they had left, "They're taking some of your best old furniture and that old trunk your grandmother brought from England. Are you just going to let them?" I don't remember exactly what I said at the time, but I do remember it wasn't but a few days later that I met with Ralph's attorney, Bill Bennett, and revised the will. Got to keep things as even as possible and then they can fight over the rest; if they want to, that is, and I'm sure that Reba will stake her claim. Never said anything to me but I knew. How could she not think I'd find out, and from one of her own children no less, what she said a few months back — something awful like 'I'll be glad when the old lady is gone." Something about then being able to get her kitchen remodeled. Well, all I can say is she's just going to have to wait for that remodeling job. Yes sir.

Oh my! That remark really hurt. I can't remember if that was before or after we found out she had sold the old trunk. Doesn't matter though, does it? All that's gone now. Time to look forward. Not for me to worry any more.

Oh, look over there at Mikie. Don't cry now Mikie — oh how he hated for me to call him Mikie — I tried to stop, but Michael just seemed so formal. Please don't cry now Mikie. This is so hard on him, what with us being so close and all, but Sally will help him through it. What a gem she is. Just like she's my own daughter. Sat there every night the last two weeks holding one of my hands while my sweet dear Cathy held the other, each taking turns reading my favorite poems. I know how tired they were. Night after night. I could see the exhaustion.

Speaking of Cathy, where is she? Wait! You can't start without my Cathy. Where is she? I see the boys but I don't see Cathy. Oh my goodness. Look, there she is lighting the candles and just as beautiful as the day she was born. And isn't that a beautiful pink dress? How in the world did my baby girl get to be fifty-eight years old? How could I ever forget that year? Being alone and worried all the time. Good thing we had the Ranch which really was more a farm, but Grandmother and Grandfather liked the sound of the word "Ranch" and so that's what they called our beloved fifty acres in Southern Maryland, "Sayre Ranch" after her family back in England. It seems like it all was just yesterday.

War is so terrible. Ralph had gotten leave for two weeks — just enough time for us to try to catch up and make another baby. He didn't get to see her until the war was over. Times were hard then. Money wasn't so easy to come by. Not so today. Things are different.

They'll all have it easier now, once the estate is all settled. I just hope Randy and Reba don't contest. Bill Bennett said it's quite possible. But I hope they don't. There's enough to go around. Ralph took care of that and wasn't that just like him, always thinking of others before himself. My goodness, I hope our little plan isn't too harsh.

Now just listen to Reverend Manning. All those nice things he's saying. Why, I could say the same about him. If there ever was a saint, it's Reverend Manning even if he's the slowest man on this green earth. Can't begin to remember all the times he's pulled me through even when life wasn't being too kind to him. He's always been there for the Sayre's. All right, Reverend Manning, you know how I used to cut short my talks when I was the guest speaker? Now isn't the time for long testimonials. But those really are nice things to hear, if I do say so myself. If I didn't know him to be an honest man, I'd think he was exaggerating more than just a little bit. How sweet of him to come by last night, even though he had spent the entire day driving back from Boston. Always giving. Not a selfish bone in his body. Just like Ralph. I wish Randy had been more like his dad.

I know Randy didn't mean to be greedy but what he did, with the furniture and the trunk and all, wasn't fair to Mikie and Cathy. Looking back on it, I guess I should have called him and Reba on it right then and there before that truck got out of the driveway, but I don't like confrontations. Never did. Not even when he took over my bank account and started calling my doctor and making those decisions for me too. I know he means well but I hope he never has to lose control of his life, not able to drive or manage his own money or have a say in any of his own affairs. My goodness, I do love him just like the others, yet I wonder what he'll do when he doesn't have me to boss around and Reba will tell him what to do and when to do it and they won't be able to spend their share right away.

So many children in the front two rows. My, my, I've lost track of the grandchildren. At last count, I think it was seven and I believe Cathy told me there were now ten great-grandchildren and, oh yes, I mustn't forget my first great-great-grandchild little Miss Ashley born just last week. I do regret that I wasn't able to hold her not even once. I can understand why though, what with that awful cough I've had. How proud Ralph would be if he were here today to see them all in church.

Thank heavens Reverend Manning has stopped talking. Enough is enough! Why I do believe that's Mary McDaniels and she looks like she's going to sing. I had forgotten what a beautiful voice she has — just like an angel. What in the world ... ? Oh my! Only Cathy knew that's one of my favorites. Pretty soon there won't be a dry eye in the place. Except mine of course.

Well, for heaven's sake. In the back of the church, right behind the Moore's and the Johnson's. It's Bill and Lena Bennett. How nice of them to come. Well, of course they would come. Bill has been our attorney for over thirty years. Or is it forty?

He's a sharp one that Bill, bringing in three witnesses last month when we revised the will. Who would have ever thought to have that many witnesses and one a psychiatrist from Baltimore come down to attest to my soundness of mind? "Just in case anyone decides to contest the will, Helen," I remember him saying and of course when he said that my mind went right to Randy and Reba who I'm sure are going to be very unhappy at the reading. Oh, I know it sounds like a trite thing to do but — and I don't want to cut them out — but — I hope Ralph doesn't mind.

Oh my, that song was just beautiful. If I could only tell Cathy how beautiful it was. Wait! The service is almost over! They've got to get me back to McElvey's before noon. My, I hope the ride over isn't as rough as it was this morning. I knew we were driving over Cushing Lane — biggest potholes in town, big enough for a Sherman tank to fall into.

Now hold on, boys, don't let your Nana fall. My, I'm glad this thing is padded, not that I'd bruise or feel anything anyway. But just the same. Such strong, handsome sons and grandsons, all of them. I'm going to miss them terribly. I certainly hope they don't go back over Cushing Lane. Well, soon it all will be behind us and we can get on with it. Just a quick stop at McElvey's and then on to the Ranch.

At first, Bill didn't think I should go through with my plan, but when I explained my reasons, and I do think they certainly are valid and I think Ralph would agree with me, Bill went along. Only he and my dear Cathy know and Lord knows she will have to take the heat from Reba. Oh dear, I hope I'm up to taking the heat today.

It's nice to see them all together, riding in the same car, with my Cathy holding me in her lap — I knew I'd find a good use for that colorful vase she brought me back from Spain — and isn't it wonderful, they're all being quite jovial. I can't remember when we were all together at the Ranch. Was it when we spread Ralph's ashes on the lake?

My goodness, that was so long ago. I just don't remember. What a special occasion today is and more fun to come this afternoon. I haven't swum in the lake for years.

Cathy is sworn to secrecy. I hope Randy understands. It wasn't done out of malice. She will just have to be stoic if they fuss. I can hear Bill now, with them all gathered in his beautiful office, him sitting behind that massive mahogany desk and the children sitting in the three green upholstered chairs facing him, perhaps dreading the formality of the reading. The offspring of Helen and Ralph Sayre listening as the family lawyer gets to the part that will cause quite a hush in the room, followed most probably by a loud gasp. "A trust of twenty-thousand dollars has been set aside for each of my beloved grandchildren and each great-grandchild."

They will all sigh and say, "How nice." And my Cathy will glance over at Mikie and grin as Bill continues. "I bequeath ten thousand dollars to my church, Beldan Street Methodist." Reba will give a sigh of relief when she realizes that they only have to share ten thousand dollars with the church. Bill will try not to smile as he looks over at Cathy and Mikie and continues. "The remainder of my estate will be split equally in the following manner between my beloved children, Randolph, Michael, and Cathy."

Oh dear, we've arrived at the Ranch already, haven't we. What with me daydreaming, that little trip didn't take long at all. My Cathy holding me, walking slowly. There are tears again. No, my sweet little girl. I'm happy now. Please don't cry. Down the lovely path under the grape arbor laden with the juicy muscadines. It's been so long since I came down the path.

Floating. My, what a wonderful, wonderful feeling. Please, everyone. Be happy! This is what I've waited for so long. This is what I dreamed about as I sat on the side of the lake in my wheelchair, wondering what it would be like to float in the cool breeze, settling softly on the water, letting the ripples carry me along, finding Ralph again. No more pain. What a grand feeling it will be! No heavy, sick body to carry around. How delightful. Just floating in the wind and settling softly on the water. How very delightful.

Cathie and Mikie, please don't cry. And there's Randy, looking stern and sad and yes, I do believe there's a tear.

Oh my goodness, where was I? Oh yes, I remember, I was thinking about the will. "... the remainder will be split...Blah! Blah! Blah! ... in the following manner ..." I'm sure Ralph would approve of Mikie being the Executor. Randy will just have to get over it.

●●●

Oh dear, everyone's hands are so cold. Maybe it's the breeze. Floating. Floating. How wonderful! Oh I hope I've done the right thing. I'm sure I did, yes, I'm sure I did. Reba can just wait five years to get her hands on the money. They'll both just have to get over it. Getting a fifth of their share every year is better than getting nothing at all, that's what I say.

Oh dear, the water is so cool. I'd forgotten just how cool it could be in the fall. Ralph! Ralph! Oh my goodness. Is that you? It *is* you, isn't it? What did you say? Come closer, Ralph.

HOME SWEET HOME

Oh my dear, you haven't changed at all. Thank heavens you're here. Come closer, I can't hear you. Oh, the pond. Yes my love, I promise. The pond will forever be our *home-sweet-home*.

ABOUT THE AUTHOR

Virginia Saalman began her writing career as the Sports Editor of her high school newspaper in her home town of Washington, D.C. After a 35-year career with the Federal Government, she formed Great Scott Training, a management training and consulting business. During the 1980's she wrote "Leslie" a novel that never found its way into publication. In 1990 she published *Virginia Scott Speaks*, which dealt with workplace management issues.

After moving to southwest Florida in 1998, she began studying the short story craft with the late author and movie critic Hollis Alpert who was best known, perhaps, for his books: *The Life and Times of Porgy and Bess*, *The Barrymores* (1964), and *Fellini: A Life* (1986). He co-wrote autobiographies with actors Richard Burton and Charlton Heston. He was also a contributor to the *Saturday Review*, fiction editor for the *New Yorker*, and co-founder of the National Society of Film Critics.

From 1999 through most of 2005, Saalman served as Assistant and then Manager of the Museum of the Everglades in Everglades City, Florida. This historic town is the gateway to the Ten Thousand Islands and the Western entrance to Everglades National Park.

Four stories in *Frog Poop* received Honorable Mention in *Byline Magazine* writing contests: "Silent Night," "Home Sweet Home," "Jack Be Nimble, Jack Be Dead" and "Playground Open for the Summer".

Saalman lives in Naples, Florida, with her husband, Bill. Visit her website at: www.frogpoop.com.